Johnny Copper and the Case of the Missing Chocolate

Enjoy reading this fun mystery from local author, Greg Heist!

Complete the following questions and mail to

BBBS c/o Jaime Keller, 130 W. 5th Street, Davenport, IA 52801 to win a prize!

1. What were the main clues that helped solve the crime?

2. Who spotted one of the suspects at the scene of the crime? What did he see? Could he have been a suspect?

3. Who stole the chocolate? _____

D0921051

JOHNNY COPPER
and
The Case of the Missing Chocolate

Gregory S. Heist

Johnny Copper and
The Case of the Missing Chocolate
Copyright © 2012
Gregory S. Heist

Cover art by Leo Kelly

Edited by Jane VanVooren Rogers

ISBN: 978-0-615-65301-3

Copper Kids Project

Printed in the USA by
Maquoketa Web Printing
1287 East Maple Street
Maquoketa, Iowa 52060
563-652-4971
www.maqweb.com

Acknowledgements

Special thanks go out to many people that helped me along the way in writing my first children's book. Thanks to my wife, Diane, who always stands by me when I express my eagerness to try new challenges. To my two sons, Ryan and Kurt, who encourage me to write, and who make me proud to be their father. To my niece Shannon, who gave me valuable advice regarding my writing style. To my friend Jan, who helped me understand how young readers want a story to unfold. Finally, thanks to my two great-nieces, Madi and Chloe, who reviewed one of my early drafts when they were just in the third grade. Their youthful advice was refreshing.

CONTENTS

1

It was the second week of September, and class started in the morning with a wonderful surprise.

"I'm delighted to have Jim Walker, from the zoo, with us today. He is going to talk to us about one of his favorite animals," Ms. Williams announced with a smile, as Mr. Walker patiently waited just outside the door. She waved him in.

Jim walked into class, and the kids were wondering what wonderful wild animal he would be bringing with him today.

"Hi, kids! How are you today?" Jim asked as he tried to raise the level of anticipation a little bit, but all the kids sat quiet. He did not seem to have an animal with him.

Was he hiding it? Was it so small that he had it in his pocket? Where and what was this thing?

The kids looked over by the doorway to see if an animal would follow him in, but nothing entered.

"Nobody answered me! Let's try it again. How are you kids today?" Jim asked, just a little louder.

"Great, Mr. Walker!" the kids shouted almost in unison. Some of the kids noticed that Ms. Williams had slipped out into the hallway while Mr. Walker talked to them for a while.

"Has anyone ever seen one of these?" All of the students' eyes lit up, and they gave a soft, low mumble. This must have been the cue for Ms. Williams to come into the room. She walked into class carrying a small cage, which held a beautiful and silky-smooth haired … who knew what?

"I want to introduce you to Susie. She is a ring-tailed mongoose," Mr. Walker called out.

The kids were really excited to see the mongoose and they all seemed to immediately move forward in their seats to get a closer look.

During the first week of September the students had gotten to see a huge python snake and also a chubby, needle-filled porcupine. The snake was long and thick, and it turned out to be much smoother to the touch than it appeared. Well, at least according to the students who were brave enough to pet him. Needless to say, the porcupine was not the type of animal that any of the students were allowed to pet. The six-inch pointy spines did not look very inviting to gently brush your hand across. After learning about the python snake and the bristling porcupine the first week, the kids were happy that Mr. Walker brought in something a little more cuddly and lovable.

"Since Susie loves children so much, the zoo has agreed to do something they have not done before," Mr. Walker announced.

Ms. Williams stepped in front of the cage and began to speak. "The zoo has been very impressed with the wonderful students in this class. They would like us to take care of Susie, here in our classroom, for the next four weeks."

The students got very excited and some even started to scream with joy. Susie the mongoose got a little scared because of the classroom commotion, and she curled up, shaking, in the corner of her cage.

"Everyone, quiet now! We are scaring our new little friend. We don't want her to be afraid of us, do we, kids?" Ms. Williams took control of the class again. "Please, listen up. For the next hour, Mr. Walker is going to teach us about where Susie comes from and all of the important duties necessary to take care of her for the next several weeks."

The kids sat quietly, anticipating Mr. Walker's *how to take care of a mongoose* lecture. You could feel the pent up excitement building in the room, like a child waiting to open a birthday present.

Ms. Williams was considered one of the best teachers in the entire school. During the month of September, she intended on teaching the kids all about wild-life in the great outdoors. Her plan was to have guest speakers from the local zoo come to her class for several weeks and talk about the various wild animals that her students were not likely to see around their own neighborhoods. Ms. Williams hoped this would be a very informative month of teaching. The next several weeks could either be a fun learning experience, or more work than she bargained for. Ms. Williams already had two turtles and a guinea pig in her room. She was not sure if the timing was right for the children to take care of one more animal. Ms. Williams was worried that having Susie in the classroom could be a new distraction for some of the kids. She knew her main responsibility as a teacher was making sure all of her students received the best education. Having their full attention was very important.

2

As the weeks passed, taking care of Susie became quite easy for most of the students. They seemed to catch on quickly to Susie's every need. Perhaps she was just easy to please. Ms. Williams paid very little attention to her, since she was so well behaved and the class took such good care of her.

Unfortunately, for Ms. Williams, an unusual and strange development had been occurring in her classroom, which concerned her. She was troubled about recent thefts in her room. Not only was there more than one theft, but also, to make matters worse, the items were being taken from Ms. Williams' purse. She did not want to believe that any of her students would steal from her, but she was saddened by the possibility. Even more disappointing was the fact that the items being stolen were Ms. Williams' favorite chocolate bars.

Ms. Williams knew these thefts had to come to a stop, but she was not sure what to do. She did not want to make a major case out of stolen chocolate and was hoping that whoever was behind these thefts would just quit before they were caught in the act. Regrettably, her hope wasn't coming true.

What could be done to stop these thefts? Ms. Williams struggled with this question every night before going to bed. Her decision finally became clear. She decided to have the theft cases investigated. This was not an investigation for the FBI or the local police, but she also knew the principal would not want her to handle the investigation on her own. Ms. Williams made up her mind. This was a case for her favorite detectives, Johnny Copper and Carly Cruz. Johnny and Carly were not only the best detectives she ever knew, but they were also her favorite students in the entire school.

Johnny Copper was no typical kid. He was almost 4 feet 2 inches tall and tipped the scale at a whopping 65 pounds. He had straight, reddish-blonde hair and a clean, smooth face. He looked about 2 years younger than he really was. His mother told him that someday he would be glad that he looked young, but he was not buying it now, and wished he had an older, rougher look to his face. One thing very noticeable on Johnny was his thick, black framed glasses. These glasses seemed to become a trademark for Johnny. He was not very athletic by most standards, but he enjoyed watching sports and knew a lot about most of them. Johnny did enjoy three things most of all in his life: reading books, playing chess and sitting down at his piano. He lived with his mother and father and one older sister, in a simple two-story, white-framed house that sat on the corner of Main and Cherry Street.

Johnny's sister was already in college, because she was almost 8 years older than him. As far as Johnny's sister went, he would say that she was very mature and way too smart for her own good. She dreamed of becoming a doctor someday. Johnny was well loved by his family and they were often curiously, but pleasantly, surprised by his intelligence and common sense, which was way beyond his years.

Carly Cruz, on the other hand, was from a different mold than Johnny. As people often say, opposites attract. And although they were not boyfriend and girlfriend, Johnny and Carly were true, inseparable buddies. Great partners perfectly describe these two, and both were very interested in good old-fashioned detective work. Carly was a little tomboyish. She was already 5 feet 2 inches tall, with a slender, muscular body. She had jet-black hair, beautiful brown eyes and was on her way to becoming an adorable young lady. Carly did not pay much attention to her own looks, but she was hard to ignore. Her legs were long — almost to Johnny's chest — and she could outrun every single boy in school. And just like Johnny's glasses, Carly was sporting her own little trademark: a small hearing aid in her left ear. As a toddler, she'd had a very high fever, which caused some hearing loss. It never bothered her though, and it certainly never bothered Johnny. He never considered those sorts of things when it came to choosing friends. He loved Carly for her positive, straightforward attitude.

Carly was not quite the smartest girl in school, at least not in a book smart way, but her common sense and reasoning ability were the things that made her stand out. She was definitely mature beyond her years. Carly was what Copper called, a no-nonsense girl, always straight to the point. She and Johnny had one thing in common, and that was a special sensitivity to the needs of those around them. These two kids might seem like opposites, but two attributes attracted them to each other. They were both curious and most of all, they always tried to do the right thing. Ms. Williams knew that if this case could be solved, these two were the ones to do it.

It was a Friday afternoon and the last class was complete. Ms. Williams passed Johnny in the hallway and slipped a note into his backpack.

"I have an important case for you, Johnny. Look at the note I placed in your backpack when you get home," whispered Ms. Williams. "It will tell you what to do."

Johnny packed up the rest of his books from his locker and headed out of the school. He made it home and darted straight for his bedroom to look at Ms. Williams' note. The note requested Johnny look at an email she had sent him, but he decided to make an important phone call first. He dialed the phone number without hesitation.

"Is Carly home?" Johnny asked. "I really have to talk to her now."

"Yes, Johnny. I'll get her. She just walked in the door," Carly's mom replied.

Johnny was very anxious. "Sorry to be so impatient, Mrs. Cruz, but I really have to talk to Carly."

"That's OK. She's on her way to the phone. It'll just be a minute. She's still dropping her backpack in her room," Mrs. Cruz explained.

"Hi, Copper," Carly answered, pausing just for a second. "Hold on a minute."

Carly yelled down the stairs to the kitchen. "Mom, you can hang up now. I got it!" Mrs. Cruz hung up the phone.

"Copper, what in the world is going on?" Carly asked. "You sound really excited about something."

"I think we might have another case. Ms. Williams gave me a note before I left school today," Johnny said. "Her note said that she sent me an email. I just opened it."

"What does it say, Copper?" Carly yelled.

"She says that there have been thefts occurring at school. She has listed all of the details. I'm on my laptop right this minute checking it out. Do you want to come over and see what kind of case we have?" Johnny asked. He was really excited, because the investigating duo had not had a good case for about two months.

11

Carly hung up the phone and jumped on her bike to head over to Johnny's house. She was at his house within a few minutes. After all, she only lived about three blocks away. She ran straight inside his house. They were such good friends that, neither one of them ever knocked when they visited each other. Carly flew up to Johnny's room. She plopped down on a chair, excited about their new case. They both anticipated reading the list of facts that Ms. Williams wrote in her email.

Carly looked to Johnny for a hint as to what was going on. "What do we have this time, Copper?"

"Looks like a theft case of some kind," Johnny said, rubbing his hands together. He loved solving theft cases. But as he read further, this one seemed a little trickier than those they had investigated in the past.

"Ms. Williams is really upset about this one," Johnny noted. "It appears as though there have been at least three thefts within the past two and a half weeks and she was very reluctant to have them investigated."

"We know that once a suspect finds an easy target, they come back, over and over again," Carly reminded Johnny.

"You got that right," Johnny agreed as he continued to read. "This one makes me mad, Carly. The thefts are happening right in our classroom!" Johnny screeched.

"I feel like we are as much victims as Ms. Williams," Carly said.

Both kids studied Ms. Williams' email for all the details. The following facts filled the computer screen:

1.   Three thefts have occurred in the last two and a half weeks from my classroom.

2. The thefts are occurring from the exact same place, my purse.

3. My purse has always been out of sight, high upon a shelf, and out of reach.

4. The thief only takes my chocolate bar, but not my money.

5. I have not noticed any evidence left behind.

6. I believe the thefts have occurred between noon and 1 o'clock.

7. I hate to suspect any of my students, but it is hard to believe another teacher would be doing this. Which student could it be?

Ms. Williams' email message was complete. "That is all for now," she wrote. "If you choose to take this case, thank you very much. If you decide not to take the case, please reply to this email, and I will understand. Thanks for your help, Johnny."

"Is this all we have, Copper?" Carly wondered. "Do we have any suspects?"

"It doesn't look like it," Johnny replied, shaking his head. "There has to be some kind of evidence in that classroom," Johnny asserted. "Let's think about what might be in that room that can help us. If there is any evidence in that room, we need to find it. Are you with me on this case, Carly?" Johnny asked.

"I'm in, Copper!" she replied as the two stood up and high-fived. "So what's our next step?"

Johnny just grinned and began to walk away, waving for Carly to follow. "Come with me, and I'll show you."

3

Johnny invited Carly to the basement of his house for a fascinating surprise. The two detectives headed down the long stairway.

"My dad let me have this old crime scene kit filled with all the tools we'll need," Johnny said. Carly was excited.

"Great! Let's take a look and see what we have," Carly replied, as she reached for a magnifying glass, holding it up to her eye. She was always interested in crime scene evidence and the tools that technicians used for their job.

Johnny Copper's dad, also named John, was a well-known detective in town. All of the officers at the department called him J.C., and he was well respected as a criminal investigator. It sure seemed like Johnny Jr. was following right in dad's footsteps and loved solving crimes too.

"Look at all this stuff we have, Carly. We can use this for sure," Johnny said.

"Wow, what is this stuff?" Carly asked as she held up a jar of shiny, black powder.

"That's volcanic powder. Dad says it sticks to fingerprints," Johnny responded. "That will really come in handy."

"I just hope we can find some fingerprints in Ms. Williams' classroom," Carly said. "How does this volcanic stuff work?"

Johnny then pulled out a curious tool from the kit. It resembled a small paintbrush. The handle was about seven inches long and had a bunch of soft nylon hair-like bristles on the opposite end. They were light and billowy. The handle was made of maple, and was less than a quarter-inch thick. It was very easy to maneuver, similar to a long pencil.

"See this special brush?" Johnny coached. "This is used to dip into the jar of black volcanic powder."

Carly picked up one of the brushes in the kit and began to twist and turn and paint the air like a marching band conductor. "Cool!"

"You need a very soft brush like this to gather the volcanic powder and gently spread it over the invisible fingerprints," Johnny said. "First you gently dip the brush into the powder jar. Don't forget to shake off the excess. Then you lightly brush over the area that you believe contains an invisible fingerprint."

Carly handed Johnny a glass from which she had been drinking her soda. "Show me how to do it on this, Copper." You could not see any of Carly's fingerprints on the glass. They were completely invisible, but she knew they had to be there.

Johnny took the glass and laid it on its side, directly on top of Mr. Copper's workbench. "You are about to see your fingerprints appear on this glass, just like magic, in less than one minute," Johnny proclaimed. He dipped the nylon brush into the jar of volcanic powder. The pretty white flowing bristles were now tipped with black powder. Johnny shook them to knock off the excess, and he began to whisk the brush all over the sides of the glass, from one end to the other. As he did this, he began to watch for Carly's fingerprints to appear on the clean, smooth glass surface. "Look right there," Johnny told Carly. "That's your thumbprint."

"Keep going, Copper," Carly encouraged. "I want to see a black image of my entire hand appear around that glass."

Johnny continued the process until all five of her fingerprints began to slowly show up on the glass, one by one, right before their eyes.

"How does that work, Copper?" Carly asked. "That's neat."

"Well, from what dad tells me, our bodies give off oil that sticks to many things. We just can't see it. The oil is pretty much invisible, just like our prints," Johnny lectured.

"So, what you're saying is that the black powder sticks to our body's oils and turns the invisible to visible," Carly confirmed. She caught on very quickly. That's why Johnny loved having her as a partner.

"Hey, Copper, just think of all the fingerprints we leave behind on our phones, video games, books and everything else we have in the house," Carly giggled.

"No kidding. If the oils we left behind were black, instead of invisible, everything we owned would look like a mess," Johnny laughed.

Carly joined in after she had a funny thought. "You've seen my brother's appetite. Wow! Our refrigerator would be completely black with his fingerprints as much as he visits the kitchen."

"Yeah, but it sure would make it much easier to follow him around," Johnny joked.

"Okay, Copper, now that you found my fingerprints on the glass, what do we do with them?" Carly asked.

Johnny got out a package of fingerprint tape tabs, which are small square tabs of tape used to lift the black fingerprints from the smooth surface of the glass. He removed one of the tape tabs, peeled off the protective backing, so the sticky side was exposed, and then placed it down flat on top of one of Carly's fingerprints. He firmly pressed down on the tape tab, rubbing it with his finger, back and forth, to make sure he had the entire fingerprint covered by the tape. Johnny then slowly pulled up on the tape tab, lifting the print right off of the glass. Carly's fingerprint was now stuck to the sticky side of the tape.

"Take a look at that, Carly. That fingerprint belongs to you and no other person in the world has a print like that. It's one of a kind. It's yours and yours alone," Johnny said.

"Are you sure there's not another match somewhere in the world, Copper?" Carly pondered.

"Absolutely not," Johnny replied. "At least that's what dad told me."

"So, now what do you do with this black print on the tape? Where do you put it? How do we save it?" Carly asked.

"Now we save the print by placing it on a notecard. You know, just like the ones we use in class when we do book reports." Johnny showed her.

He pulled out a package of notecards. Carly noticed that one side of the card was slightly rough to the touch, but the other side was extremely smooth, and shiny, like the surface of an ice skating rink. Johnny laid the card down flat on the table and took the tape tab, which contained the fingerprint, and smoothly pressed it against the glossy side of the card. "This card's slippery surface is going to help the fingerprint look much clearer, once the tape tab is pressed down onto it."

Carly watched with amazement.

"This will preserve it forever," said Johnny. "It will also make it much easier to look at the fingerprint under a magnifying glass."

"That's cool," Carly exclaimed. "Criminals better watch out now. We've learned something new!" She wondered what their next step would be in this investigation. "What is our next plan of attack, Copper?"

Johnny laid out what he hoped would be a good strategy. "Well, first we're going to track down any potential witnesses to the crime and do some interviews. Second, we'll check directly around the crime scene in Ms. Williams' room for any fingerprints. Finally, we'll talk to Ms. Williams about setting up an undercover camera in the classroom and lure the suspect back for more chocolate."

"So, we're going to secretly place another candy bar in Ms. Williams' purse and try to catch the culprit on video?" Carly wondered.

"Sounds like a plan to me," Johnny said. "I don't think our suspect can resist the sweet taste of chocolate."

Carly looked over at a clock on the wall above Mr. Copper's workbench and climbed up the stairs toward home. She realized that she was running late for dinner. "See you, Copper!" she yelled as she sprinted, at least two stairs at a time, toward the front door of the house.

Johnny slowly made it to the front door, stepping outside onto the stoop, shouting, "See you at school tomorrow, Carlita!"

As she sped across the street on her bike she came to a dead stop, turned around, and looked back at Johnny with a piercing glare. She smiled and gave him a thumbs up. Carly knew Johnny was only teasing with her when he called her Carlita, which was actually her given name. She felt a little uneasy about her tomboy image, and there were times when Johnny joked with her about it, calling her Carlita. All the kids at school called her Carly. Only her grandparents and parents ever called her Carlita. She knew how much Johnny liked her as a friend, so she only gave him half-hearted warnings when he did it.

Johnny knew that Carly was the best detective partner he could ever have, and nothing could hurt their friendship. He shut the front door and ran up to his room, settling into his computer chair. Johnny opened his email again and began to review the clues to their new and unusual case of the missing chocolate. He read over the facts that Ms. Williams provided one more time.

4

Early the next morning class started, and Johnny had a problem keeping focused on his studies. After all, he was sitting in the middle of a potential crime scene. He kept looking around the classroom for clues. One thing Johnny definitely noticed was how high the shelf was where Ms. Williams kept her purse.

"Boy, this suspect had to be quite a good climber to reach her purse," he whispered to himself. "I am going to have to check out that shelf for fingerprints. No one could climb up there without leaving some sort of print evidence." Johnny continued to daydream about the investigation. He also wondered, as he quietly scanned the room, which student had the motive to commit such crimes.

Carly slipped Johnny a small note on the back of a gum wrapper that she had found in her desk. It read: "Copper, I figured out a great place for a hidden camera if we decide to use one." He folded up the wrapper and placed it in his shirt pocket. Johnny winked at her through his thick-glassed lenses and all of a sudden the bell rang, startling them both.

Because of all his daydreaming, the class passed by quickly. Johnny put everything into his backpack and stood up to leave, when he received a tap on his shoulder. Ms. Williams was standing there and handed him his test back. *Very Nice* was written in bright red ink at the top of the test.

"Great job on the test, Johnny," Ms. Williams stated. Attached with a paper clip to his test was a short handwritten note. All it contained was the following: "Possible suspect…Billy. Talk to witness, the janitor,

Mr. Miller. He may have seen something that will interest you." Nothing more was written or said about the note.

Johnny politely addressed his teacher. "Thanks for the 'A' on my test and the nice words." The note Ms. Williams left him raised his level of interest in this case even more. For once they had a possible suspect to investigate. Johnny headed toward his locker, and he could not wait to catch up with Carly to give her the news about their first real lead.

Johnny caught up to Carly by the time she reached her locker. The two investigators talked in the hallway before having to go to their next class. Johnny handed her the note with the new lead. "Look at this, Carly."

She read the note quickly and with a look of surprise, Carly questioned Johnny. "Do you really suspect a kid like Billy of this sort of crime?"

"I don't know, but we can't ignore it. We will have to talk with the janitor, Mr. Miller. I know that for sure," said Johnny.

"So, do you think he saw something suspicious or what?" Carly wondered as she continued with her thoughts. "He may have seen Billy somewhere in the area of Ms. Williams' classroom during the time of one of the thefts. Hey, Copper, I see Mr. Miller every day at 3 o'clock after my last class, on my way to my locker. Do you want me to talk to him? I can still do it today."

Johnny agreed that Carly's suggestion was a good idea. At least they would have more details as to what the janitor had witnessed.

"Let's meet tonight and you can tell me what Mr. Miller had to say to you." Johnny looked at his watch and continued toward his locker. "I have to get home quickly after school for my piano lesson. It starts at 4 o'clock, and I have to be home early to practice for a little bit. Come over to my house after 6 o'clock tonight," Johnny instructed, with an urgent sound in his voice. He took off, making his way down the hallway.

When it came to Johnny's piano lesson, nothing stood in his way. Even though Johnny enjoyed the piano, it was his mother that demanded a good musical upbringing for her children. Mrs. Copper could really play the piano well, almost as good as a classical pianist.

Later on, at about six-thirty, Carly arrived at Johnny's house. She barged straight in, practically running into Johnny's father as he was leaving. "Hi Mr. C," she said with a little awkwardness.

"How are you young lady?" Mr. Copper asked.

"I'm fine. Is Johnny here?" Carly asked, clearly in a hurry.

"He sure is. Let me go get him."

Johnny had been finishing his homework, but anticipated Carly's visit, so he ran straight to the door. "What's up, Carly? What did you learn from Mr. Miller?"

"You won't believe it," Carly answered. "We just may have ourselves a good suspect." Johnny was waiting attentively for her opinion, as they ran up the stairs to his room.

"Billy may be our guy," Carly said in shock. "If he's not a good suspect, then he sure is a good witness."

"Why do you say that?" Johnny asked, pushing Carly for more details.

"Hold on a second," Carly replied as she took a deep breath before she answered. "Mr. Miller saw Billy coming out of Ms. Williams' classroom on the day of one of the thefts."

Johnny was stunned at first with disbelief. "You're kidding. Are you sure?" Johnny asked, somewhat saddened by the news.

"Well, I can't be sure yet, but Billy is our one and only lead right now," Carly told Copper. "We can't ignore Mr. Miller's information."

"What is the evidence? What did Mr. Miller see? Talk to me, Carly!" Johnny demanded.

"Patience, patience," she scolded. "When you get all excited, Copper, you don't think straight!" Carly stated, sounding more like Johnny's mother rather than his friend.

"OK, I get the message. Where do we go from here?" Johnny asked.

"One of us will definitely have to talk to Billy. The janitor saw him coming out of the classroom during recess, at 12:30, when no one is even supposed to be in the school," Carly clarified. "According to Mr. Miller, Billy came out of the room with a frightened look on his face and was holding onto a wrapper," Carly said with some sadness in her voice. "It appeared to be the wrapper from a chocolate candy bar."

Johnny was bewildered by this eyewitness evidence and was still soaking in the information from their new lead. Johnny began to stroke his chin as he removed his thick, black-framed glasses. He cleaned them on his favorite T-shirt. "Huh! Billy? That just doesn't sound like the Billy I know," Johnny admitted to himself. "Maybe I'm wrong, but this doesn't feel right, Carly."

"Remember, Copper, anything is possible," Carly said. "We've got to follow all of the leads."

"Yeah, I know, but Billy doesn't seem like the kind of kid that would steal chocolate from Ms. Williams." Johnny tried to make sense of his doubt.

"Why do you say that?" Carly asked.

"I've known Billy a long time, and I guess I just don't want to believe he would be so selfish that he would steal from our teacher," Johnny said.

"Don't get soft on me now, Copper. We have a suspect, and you can't let your emotions get in the way of following up our first lead!" Carly asserted. "Anyone is capable of making a mistake."

"I'm aware of that, but it's not just my emotions that I'm considering here," Johnny tried explaining. "I have one other reason for the way I'm thinking."

"Oh, yeah. What's that?" Carly wondered.

"I have one fact we just can't ignore."

"Get to the point, Copper. I have to get home for dinner," Carly pressed.

"I don't mean to make fun of Billy," Johnny hesitated, "but do you realize how chunky he is?"

"That's rude, Copper," Carly said. "This is no time to discuss Billy's weight problem."

"I don't mean it in a bad way, but maybe this is exactly the right time to discuss his weight problem," Johnny argued. "Billy is just too heavy to make that climb up to the shelf where Ms. Williams had her purse."

Johnny's comment about Billy's weight turned out to be a pretty good defense for his friend. "You've seen Billy. He can barely make it up one flight of stairs from the gym to our classroom without stopping for oxygen."

"Copper, you're forgetting two important facts that also have something to do with Billy's weight problem," stated Carly. "First, we know he loves chocolate. Second, unless Mr. Miller is lying, he swears he saw Billy coming out of that classroom on the day of one of the thefts, with a chocolate candy bar wrapper in his hand. These are two good reasons to stay focused on Billy for now." Carly asked Johnny to walk her home, so they could keep talking about their case.

Johnny once again felt cornered. Perhaps he was trying too hard to find reasons why Billy could not have committed these crimes. It was as if he was behaving more like a good friend than a detective. "There's no getting around it. We have to interview Billy and get some answers," Johnny concluded, knowing what Carly was about to suggest.

"Yeah, you're right and you're the one to do it," Carly replied. "I interviewed the janitor. Now it's your turn to quiz our first real suspect." Carly tried to hold back a laugh. "Besides, Billy always gets shy around me, so I don't think I could get him to talk anyway."

Johnny had no choice but to accept the task at hand. "That's fine. Billy and I have chess club tomorrow night. I'll talk with him then." Johnny realized there was no way around confronting Billy. "This will finally help us figure out exactly what Mr. Miller saw that day."

Both detectives stopped at the halfway point to Carly's house, and Johnny turned to head home. He was totally absorbed now on Billy as their first suspect.

"Later, Copper," Carly said as she smiled and waved. "See you tomorrow."

"See you tomorrow, Carly," Johnny said, giving her two thumbs up. This was his way of telling her that she could count on him to have a great interview with Billy. They both stared at each other as they walked backward, getting further and further apart, waiting for the other one to turn around first. Laughter broke out as Johnny stumbled over his own feet, barely keeping his balance. They both finally turned and ran, heading toward their own homes, knowing that they had to finish their homework and think more about where this case was taking them. Johnny knew it was about to become an interesting ride.

5

Johnny and Billy arrived at the school by 6 o'clock, ready to play chess. Johnny decided to talk to Billy before other club members started arriving. "Hey Billy, I noticed the last few weeks that you've been missing from the playground during recess. What's up?" Johnny asked. "Did Ms. Williams want you to stay in the classroom during recess or is something else going on?"

"No, nothing is going on. Why do you ask?" Billy replied nervously.

"I thought I saw you through the classroom window, but it must have been someone else," Johnny suggested, knowing he really hadn't seen him at all. He seemed to be trying to give Billy an alibi. Johnny could tell that Billy was getting a little red in the face and was hiding something from him. Johnny really liked Billy and felt like he was putting him on the spot. Johnny did not seem to show the heart of a tough detective. This interrogation was not starting out very well.

"You saw me?" Billy said. "I wasn't doing anything in there. I swear!" Billy was shocked that Johnny may have seen him in the classroom. Johnny was startled too. He thought he may have just taken Billy by surprise and maybe even caught him in a big lie about why he was in Ms. Williams' classroom. Billy started to walk away from the chess table, but Johnny followed. "Hey! Stop, Billy. Where are you going?" Johnny asked, wanting to continue with his questioning.

Billy stopped abruptly and turned to Johnny as if he was about to confess something. "OK, I was in Ms. Williams' room, but I wasn't doing anything wrong!"

"Did Ms. Williams send you to her room?" Johnny asked.

"No way. Ms. Williams didn't send me in there," Billy admitted with a bright red face. "She didn't even know I left the playground. If she had, I would have gotten in a lot of trouble, for sure." Billy sounded quite frightened, as if he thought he had just blown his cover. "You won't tell her I was in there, will you Johnny?"

Johnny was not sure what to make of Billy's odd behavior. He couldn't exactly put his finger on the problem. Was this Billy's way of admitting he was in Ms. Williams' classroom to steal the chocolate? If it was, he sure wasn't coming right out and confessing. Johnny was beginning to question what Billy was doing in that classroom. Why was Billy so worried about Ms. Williams finding out he was in her room?

"How many times have you gone into Ms. Williams' classroom without her permission?" Johnny whispered, trying not to be intimidating.

"Just three or four times, but I swear I didn't do anything wrong," Billy tried to assure Johnny. Johnny could not figure out why Billy kept repeating over and over again that he had not done anything wrong. What kind of person keeps telling you he didn't do anything wrong, but still won't tell you what it was that he was doing in there? Johnny hadn't even asked Billy if he had done anything wrong, but Billy kept trying to promise Johnny that he hadn't. What was Billy hiding? As an investigator, Johnny could only read Billy's behavior three ways: First, Billy did not know anything about the missing chocolate bars. Or second, Billy was in the room doing something else that he was not supposed to be doing. Or third, Billy was totally lying and was the chocolate thief after all.

Johnny could not ignore the fact that Billy had been in the room three or four times, and three chocolate bars were stolen. The janitor, Mr. Miller, also saw Billy holding what he believed was a candy bar wrapper. Was this a coincidence or did Carly and Johnny already have the right suspect in their grasp?

"Johnny, are you going to tell on me or not?" Billy asked nervously.

"I don't have anything to say to Ms. Williams right now," Johnny told Billy as he placed his hand on his shoulder. Johnny could not bring himself to come right out and ask Billy if he had stolen the chocolate bars, so he ended the interview without even mentioning the thefts at all. Both boys went back to their table, cleared the chessboard for a new game, and began to play.

Johnny could not focus on the chess game and was lost in thought, because of what had just taken place with his friend Billy. On the one hand, Billy admitted he was at the scene of the crimes three times. On the other hand, one thing kept Johnny thinking that Billy couldn't have done it. Johnny was convinced that Billy could never have climbed up high enough to get to Ms. Williams' purse, where the chocolate was at when stolen. Billy was a solid 30 pounds overweight and couldn't even jump 2 inches off the ground, let alone climb up to that shelf. This was the key reason Johnny could not bring himself to suspect Billy.

There was one problem with Johnny's line of thinking. Johnny's dad had an old saying when talking about criminals: "When there's a will, there's a way." Johnny pondered this simple belief. Perhaps even Billy could reach the top shelf if he desired those chocolate bars badly enough. The second reason why Johnny questioned Billy as a suspect was more emotional. Johnny really liked Billy and believed he was not capable of committing the crimes of theft. He was just too nice of a kid.

After the boys completed their chess games, they headed for home. As they walked down the sidewalk, Johnny could not resist his curiosity. "Hey Billy, do you mind answering one more question for me?"

"No," Billy responded shyly. "Go ahead and ask."

Johnny looked straight into Billy's eyes. "Why were you going into Ms. Williams' classroom when you knew you were supposed to be outside at recess with the rest of the class?"

Billy answered softly. "Let's just say, I wasn't all alone. I was in there with a very good friend."

This took Johnny by surprise. "I thought you were the only person in the room. Are you telling me someone else was in the classroom with you?" Johnny inquired, confused even more.

Before he could answer, Billy's mom hollered for him to get into the house for dinner.

"I don't get it, Billy," Johnny said, getting a little upset. "Who was in that classroom with you?"

Billy ran for the front door and turned toward Johnny as he quickly entered the house. "I can't say, because I wouldn't want to get her into trouble. I have never had a friend that was so nice and cool since I started school this year."

Billy's loyalty to this unknown friend seemed unusually strong. This suggested to Johnny that they might have to look for a second suspect; possibly a girl. Billy ran into the house, and Johnny turned for home.

"What in the world was he talking about?" Johnny quietly asked himself, as he slowly walked in a mental fog toward his house.

Johnny's interview with Billy seemed to answer some questions, but unfortunately it raised one big new one. Who else was with Billy in that classroom? If that question was answered, he and Carly might be able to focus on a new suspect. If Billy was not alone in that classroom, someone else had access to that chocolate too. Johnny could not remember if anyone else was ever missing from the playground. His thoughts were racing and he really hoped for a lucky break.

Johnny caught himself talking out loud as he went into the front door of his own house. "What did Billy mean when he said he did not want to get *her* in trouble? Who is *she*? Why is he so loyal to *her*?"

"Who are you talking to, Son?" Mr. Copper asked as Johnny came into the front hallway.

"Just talking to myself, Dad," Johnny mumbled, still in a daze. "I was thinking out loud again. That's all."

"Should your mother and I be worried?" Mr. Copper asked, with a gigantic smile across his face.

"Of course not, Dad," Johnny replied as he dragged himself to his bedroom. "You know me ... always thinking out loud." Johnny grabbed the phone to call Carly and tell her about the strange interview he had with Billy. Once he got a hold of her he tried to explain the interview, but found it very difficult. His conversation with Billy seemed to have created more confusion and no real answers. Finding fingerprints at the crime scene was more important than ever, with hopes of moving the case forward. This would be a new task for the detectives tomorrow.

6

Johnny brought his fingerprint kit with him to school and kept it in his locker. If he received permission from Ms. Williams he planned on searching for some fingerprints after school when everyone was gone for the day.

When school was over, Carly met Johnny at his locker. "Is it a go, Copper?"

"We're going to do it after everyone is gone. Ms. Williams is going to be in the classroom checking papers, so she said we could come in then," Johnny said.

Both detectives headed to their classroom. Ms. Williams had already gotten a stepladder in case the kids needed it to reach the high shelf. Carly and Johnny were happy with that because they knew a ladder would come in handy if they had to stay up there and look around. The detectives immediately went to work. They climbed up near the shelf where the suspect would have had to climb to commit the thefts. Johnny noticed something interesting right away.

"Look at this, Carly," he said as he pointed to a small glass jar that was sitting a few inches away from where Ms. Williams always placed her purse. The jar had clearly been moved recently, but by whom? It sat on the shelf in a thin layer of dust. The jar contained old broken pieces of colored chalk, pencils, a few boxes of crayons and some dry erase markers.

"That's weird, Copper. I never noticed that jar there before, did you?" Carly wondered. "Are you thinking what I'm thinking?"

"Carly, do me a favor and look closely at the jar, toward the top, on the sides," Johnny directed.

Carly was taller than Johnny and was actually closer to the jar. It helped her get a better view. "I see two smudges toward the top, Copper."

"Can you tell if the smudges are just chalk, or are they fingerprints?" Johnny's keen senses were becoming noticeable in his questions.

"I think they might be fingerprints," Carly said as she started to reach for the glass jar with her bare hands.

"Stop right there, Carly!" Johnny shouted. "Don't touch that jar!"

Carly froze in place.

Johnny stepped down and away for a moment to find something to place the jar in, to protect the two fingerprints on the glass. Johnny remembered that he had a pair of old gloves in his desk, which no matter how many times his mom told him to bring them home, he forgot.

Johnny hurried and got the gloves from his desk, then reached up and handed Carly the right one.

"Put this glove on your right hand and grab the glass jar by the very top of the rim, on the opposite side of the fingerprints, and hand it down to me," Johnny instructed with tension is his voice.

Carly was slow and careful, placing the glove on her right hand, grabbing the jar where she was told, and handing the jar down to Copper. "Got it?" Carly asked.

"Got it, Carly," Johnny answered as he grabbed the jar with his left hand. Johnny had already placed the other glove on his left hand while he waited, so he would not leave his prints on the jar.

Johnny found a paper bag in Ms. Williams' closet and slipped the glass jar inside, hoping to save the two fingerprints for the trip back to his house.

Johnny was not done investigating the area around Ms. Williams' purse yet. "Carly, do you see anything on the shelf, surrounding the area of the jar, which looks like fingerprints?" Johnny questioned out loud.

"Someone has definitely touched the shelf, but there is so much dust up here, I can't see any fingerprints," Carly responded with frustration. "I don't know for sure what I'm looking at, because of all the dirt." Carly gave Johnny her best guess. "It looks like the suspect's fingers touched the shelf, moving the dust, but that's all." Carly thought for a moment. "I wonder if the suspect was wearing gloves during the thefts."

"I can't see how any fingerprints were left behind on that dirty shelf," Johnny said, now a little worried. "My tape tabs for lifting prints won't stick to anything that dusty. These shelves have not been cleaned for a long time."

"Copper, I think we've run out of luck on this shelf," Carly reluctantly admitted. "Let's hope we catch a break with those prints on the glass jar."

"You're right, let's go to my house," Johnny said. "I'm really excited about trying to remove these two fingerprints from this jar."

"This is getting exciting, Copper!" Carly said, all pumped up. "If these prints come off of this jar like the prints came off of that drinking glass that we practiced on, we might just solve this case tonight."

"Let's not get ahead of ourselves, Carly," Johnny replied, obviously concerned about what they were seeing on the side of that jar. "If these turn out to be just smudges and not actual fingerprints, we're back to square one."

Johnny and Carly headed out of the classroom. "Thanks Ms. Williams for letting us work the crime scene," Carly said. "We'll get back to you once we figure out what we have here."

"You're very welcome, kids," Ms. Williams replied as she waved to the detectives with a thankful smile. "If there is anything else I can do, just let me know." Both kids gradually began to pick up their pace, due to their excitement, as they headed down the hallway toward the school exit.

But halfway down the hallway something clicked in Carly's head. "Copper, stop for a minute. I just thought of something, and it really has me worried."

Johnny seemed a little frustrated, because it was probably the first time that he was actually a few steps ahead of her as they were sprinting out of school. It was rare that he was in the lead when they were running home.

"What's up, Carly?" Johnny said, somewhat miffed.

Carly paused, almost frozen in thought, as if she was about to drop some bad news on him. "Let's just say, for the sake of argument, we get home and we successfully remove those two prints from that glass jar."

"OK. Let's say that's what happens," Johnny replied, pushing her to get to the point. "That's what we want, right?"

"Yes, but we have nothing to compare the two fingerprints to," Carly revealed, almost startling herself with this newfound problem. "Do you see what I'm getting at, Copper?"

"You're exactly right," Johnny responded in despair. "We're going to need other people's fingerprints to compare them to." Johnny took a few seconds, trying to recall the correct name for these kinds of fingerprints. "They're called rolled prints, I think, or sometimes called elimination prints."

"What do you mean by rolled?" Carly asked.

"Rolled or elimination fingerprints are prints that we take from every student, teacher, or anyone else who may have been in that classroom near the scene of the crime," Johnny stated, shaking his head from side to side in frustration. "They call them rolled prints, because you have to roll each and every one of the person's ten fingers onto a print card." Both kids were clearly upset now.

Elimination prints were something they simply forgot about in their excitement after finding the two prints on the jar, which sat unnoticed right next to Ms. Williams' purse.

Carly was still puzzled as to their next step. "Rolled prints are like the ones the police officer did for our class a couple of years ago, right, Copper?" Carly asked as they reached the end of the hallway. He kept walking slower and slower until he stopped and sat down on a bench next to the exit door and began to plan their next move. He knew that this problem had to be solved soon.

"Honestly Carly, my head has been in a cloud trying to figure out how to clear Billy as a suspect," Johnny softly admitted. "I never once considered all the fingerprints all over that big room, which are left behind by completely innocent students, teachers and other school workers."

"Don't worry about it, Copper. Tell me what we need to do, and we'll get it done," Carly said.

Johnny began to calm himself down and think straight again. "The key to eliminating the innocent people from this case is to compare their rolled fingerprints to the prints that we hope to remove from that glass jar." Johnny looked into Carly's eyes to make sure she was following him. She stared right back at him.

"Aha! Now I get it. Just like when that police officer inked my fingers and rolled them onto that fingerprint card." Carly made it clear that she understood. "Then we would be able to compare the fingerprint card of mine to the prints we removed off of that drinking glass at your house ... the one we practiced on."

"Exactly," Johnny responded. "When you grabbed that glass you left your prints on it. Then we removed them from the glass. The next step would have been to compare those prints we took from the glass to the rolled fingerprints the police officer took from you two years earlier," Johnny lectured. "That is the only way we would know for sure that the prints on the glass were from your fingers."

Johnny's explanation had finally paid off. Their confusion was gone as to what they needed to do next.

They both stood straight up from the bench and left school. "Copper, we have no choice," Carly said, knowing what his reaction would be. "We have to roll the fingerprints of everyone in the entire class, don't we?"

"We sure do. We have no choice." Johnny looked straight ahead and kept walking.

"Can your dad get us a stack of those blank fingerprint cards?" Carly wondered, hoping Mr. Copper would come through for them again. "Like … maybe enough to do the whole class again?"

"Yes. My dad always helps out," Johnny said, reminding Carly of the difficult task ahead. "We're also going to have to get the rolled prints of Ms. Williams and the janitor, Mr. Miller."

"Ms. Williams will be easy, but I don't know how we'll convince Mr. Miller that we need his fingerprints," Carly said, sounding a little concerned.

"Don't worry about Mr. Miller, because I have an idea on exactly how to get his!" Johnny perked up and got a smile on his face. "Ms. Williams can help us out with that little problem."

"Speaking of little problems, Copper," Carly announced, "if we mess up and can't remove those two fingerprints from that glass jar, rolling everyone's prints tomorrow in class won't do us a bit of good."

"You're quite the downer, Carly," Johnny pointed out. "I feel that our luck is about to change. Those two little prints on that jar just may be the answer."

"Let's do it, Copper!" Carly stated. "I can't wait. We can remove those prints right now, in your basement." Both kids ran into Johnny's house and darted straight for Mr. Copper's workbench.

"I guess there's no reason to wait," Johnny replied, although he was obviously nervous about his true ability to remove those prints from that jar. "This is no longer practice, Carly," Johnny reminded her. "We have one chance and only one chance to get this right."

Both investigators walked to Johnny's dad's workbench. Johnny removed the glass jar from the paper bag, careful not to put any of his own fingerprints on the jar. Carly found some old newspapers to lie down on the bench, so they did not get the volcanic powder all over the place.

Carly found a pair of rubber gloves in the fingerprint kit. "Here ya go, Copper," Carly offered, acting like an experienced detective. "You'll need these before you start dusting the jar for those prints."

Johnny put the tight rubber gloves on his hands, opened the small container of black volcanic powder, and waited as Carly slowly pulled the fingerprint brush from the kit. She laughed as she waved it across the air like a symphony conductor.

Johnny reached up and grabbed it from her hand, then went to work on the glass jar. He lightly dusted the sides of the jar, to make sure he was doing it correctly. Copper was nervous and did not want to make a mistake.

"Looks like nothing but smudges, Copper," Carly noted with concern.

"Yeah, but I haven't reached the good prints yet," Johnny said, still holding onto some hope.

"Here we go," Johnny announced. He slowly swept the brush over the top side of the jar, near the opening. To both of their amazement, a thumbprint appeared like magic.

"You nailed it, Copper!" Carly shouted, somewhat startling her partner. "One more fingerprint. You can do it."

Johnny lightly ran the fine black-tipped bristles over the final print at the mouth of the jar. Just like they planned, the second fingerprint became noticeable. They could both now see the perfect pattern of someone's fingers staring back at them.

"Now the hard part," Johnny said as he reached for the packet of tape tabs. "Removing these two prints from the jar is even tougher than finding them."

"Let me do it, Copper," Carly offered with a lot of confidence in her voice.

Johnny handed her one of the tape tabs. "It's all yours, girl."

Carly placed the first tape tab over the thumbprint and firmly pushed down on the tape, so it stuck to the glass jar. She rubbed down on the tab, back and forth, to make sure she was picking up all of the black powder on the print.

"You got it Carly, but go really slow as you pull it off," Johnny said.

Carly slowly pulled, starting at one end of the piece of tape and lifting toward the other. As the tape came up off the glass jar, the black fingerprint came off of the jar and was stuck to the tape tab. Johnny was already waiting with the smooth, gleaming, notecards. Carly gently placed the tape tab down onto the notecard, pushing down with all her might.

"Rub back and forth, Carly, to make sure there are no air bubbles between the tape and the card," Johnny said.

Carly stood back away from the card when she was done, admiring her work. "I did it!" she exclaimed.

And just like a pro, she did the same thing with the second fingerprint, which was next to the mouth of the jar. They both studied the two prints closer, since they were now completely preserved on the two notecards.

"This second print looks like someone's index finger to me," Johnny guessed, since he didn't know for sure.

"Your dad will tell us, Copper," Carly replied, with a sense of relief in her voice. She was happy that she didn't ruin their best evidence in the case.

The kids ran upstairs from the basement and placed their new found fingerprint evidence in Johnny's room for safekeeping. Johnny was sure his dad would be able to tell them who left those prints on that glass jar, but only after all the rolled prints were taken tomorrow from the students in Ms. Williams' class. Without the rolled fingerprints, the two prints removed from the jar would remain a mystery.

7

The next day in class turned out to be quite interesting and fun for everyone. Johnny and Carly had already received permission from Ms. Williams for this important class project. When Ms. Williams announced to the class that all the students were going to get their fingerprints rolled again, most of the kids were excited. Many of them remembered when the local police officer did it a couple of years ago, but having Johnny and Carly try it this year was even more fun. Before the fingerprinting began, Johnny presented a short lecture about investigations and why finding fingerprints is so important to solving cases.

After his presentation, Carly took over the discussion and stood in front of the class. "We're going to do this a little different than the last time," Carly announced. "Johnny and I are going to split up the class and roll all of your fingerprints ourselves." None of the kids objected. Of course, none of them knew about the investigation, and it seemed like more fun than sitting at their desks doing homework.

Johnny pulled out two fingerprint kits with the proper print cards and black inkpads. "I will be doing all of the boys in the class, and Carly will be doing all of the girls." Carly asked all of the girls to move to one side of the room so she could begin. Johnny directed all of the boys to his side.

Carly was happy to see that Ms. Williams had stepped over to the girls' line. "I guess we're going to get to fingerprint Ms. Williams today also," Carly told the other kids.

"I thought it would be nice to compare my fingerprints to the girls', to see if there is a size difference in the prints," Ms. Williams said, always concerned about the learning process. She also knew that Carly and Johnny would be asking her for elimination prints to compare to the suspect's prints.

Carly had about eight girls' prints to roll, not counting Ms. Williams. Johnny was going to have to roll the prints of at least nine boys. All of a sudden Mr. Miller walked into the room. It seemed that Ms. Williams had invited Mr. Miller to join in on the fun, so the class would be able to compare a grown man's fingerprints with that of a young boy's. As Mr. Miller got in the boys' line, Ms. Williams looked over at Johnny and gave him a smile and wink. She knew exactly how helpful it would be to the detectives having Mr. Miller's rolled fingerprints as well. By the end of the class, Johnny and Carly rolled 19 fingerprint cards, and that included two important people, Ms. Williams and Mr. Miller.

Before the end of class, Johnny asked for one more favor of all the students. "Could everyone please sign their own name to their fingerprint card? After you're done, Carly will collect them. Once we have taken a look at each print card, we will return them next week, so you can take your own card home to your parents." Carly waited by the classroom door at the sound of the final bell and as everyone filed out, she collected all of the cards and placed them directly in her backpack.

The two detectives now had all of the rolled prints, which belonged to everyone that entered and exited their classroom every day.

"That's it, Copper," Carly said with a big smile on her face. "Now we have the rolled fingerprints we need to make a comparison to the two prints we removed from the jar."

"I'll ask my dad to make the comparison," Johnny replied, still acting nervous about something.

"What's the matter, Copper?" Carly asked, knowing her partner was uncomfortable about something.

"It's nothing, really," Johnny quietly replied. "I just don't want to get my hopes up too high over these prints."

"Whatever, Copper ... I'm out of here!" Carly grumbled as they headed for home, dashing ahead of Johnny in the blink of an eye. She was anxious for the outcome.

8

"Hey, gazelle, could you slow down and let me catch up?" Johnny jokingly screeched. "You must have the longest legs in town!"

"Listen up, Copper," Carly shot back. "You need to start doing some exercising. Your chess game and piano lessons are not helping you get into very good shape. You need to take better care of your body, not just your mind."

This was the closest thing to an argument that these two had ever had. Johnny knew Carly was right. He was so busy, he never found much time to exercise. But, he also was smart enough to know that a healthy body was important.

Carly made it to the house first, with Johnny trudging behind. They were anxious to find Mr. Copper.

Johnny's father was in the kitchen fixing a sandwich when Carly accidentally startled him. "Hi, Mr. C!" she huffed.

"Well, hello there, young lady. Where is Johnny? Pulling up the rear again?" he asked, as if he did not know Johnny would be trailing behind Carly by at least 20 feet.

"He's coming," Carly answered, somewhat sympathetic for Johnny. "He's just moving a little slow."

He came through the door and walked sluggishly into the kitchen. "Hi Dad!" Johnny said after a few deep breaths. "Dad, we have a question for you about some evidence," Johnny told his father as he continued to gasp for air.

"What did you find?" Mr. Copper wondered.

"I'll get the bag of evidence, Carly," Johnny said, running up to his room to get the notecards and glass jar, so his dad could see what they had.

"Are you two working a new case or is this still Ms. Williams' theft case?" Mr. Copper asked, as Johnny returned with the evidence.

"We're still investigating the thefts from Ms. Williams' classroom. We found two fingerprints off of a jar that was on her shelf," Carly replied as Johnny pulled the jar and prints from the bag. "We really don't know who they belong to, but we hoped you could help us."

"Dad, could you tell us who these two prints belong to?" Johnny asked politely.

"Let me see what you kids found," Mr. Copper said with curiosity. "I have to look closely at the prints to see if they are even good enough for comparison."

Mr. Copper stared at the two prints for a while and began to formulate a professional opinion. "Where did you say you found these?"

"We got them off of this little glass jar that was on the shelf in Ms. Williams' classroom," Carly told him, as she held it up for him to see.

"You two found these fingerprints on this jar and removed them without anyone's help?" Mr. Copper asked as he reached for his reading glasses. "I'm very impressed with your detective skills. That's very difficult to do."

"Yeah, Carly and I removed those prints," Johnny answered proudly. "We couldn't find prints on the shelf itself, because there was too much dust on the surface."

Mr. Copper continued to view the evidence as he adjusted his reading glasses. "I see … that happens when there is too much dust." He held the notecards up to the light, turning them upwards and then downwards and then sideways, wondering if these fingerprints were good enough to match them to a suspect.

"Interesting ... very interesting," Mr. Copper softly whispered to himself, just loud enough for the two young detectives to hear. "Uh huh.... I have a strong hunch that both of these prints are in good enough condition to identify the person who grabbed that jar," Mr. Copper told the two young investigators.

He reexamined the two fingerprints over and over again until he was satisfied. After a few more nods, moans, and groans, Mr. Copper gave his opinion. "I believe these prints may just help you solve your case, one way or another."

"What do you mean, dad?" Johnny asked.

"Well ... I'm not sure who placed these fingerprints on that jar, but they are very small," Mr. Copper concluded. "They look like a child's prints to me. I don't believe they were put on that jar by an adult, if that helps."

Johnny looked over at Carly as if a new piece of the puzzle had been solved. "Carly... this probably eliminates Mr. Miller."

Johnny's father interrupted the kids. "Did the two of you do the rolled elimination prints of all the people that go in and out of Ms. Williams' classroom?" asked Mr. Copper, hoping he did not create a new problem for the young investigators.

"Yes, we sure did," Carly came back quickly. "I thought of that already, Mr. C. We used the stack of cards you gave Copper."

"And I made sure we rolled the prints of Ms. Williams and Mr. Miller," Johnny responded, not wanting to be upstaged by Carly.

"Have you ever considered any of the girls in your class as the suspect?" Mr. Copper wondered, beginning to raise new questions.

"Are you saying these prints may have been left by a girl, dad?" Johnny asked somewhat surprised.

Carly looked at Johnny and he looked back at her as if a big light bulb just went off in his head. Carly was confused now, wondering which girl in the class may be involved. As far as she was concerned, they were back to square one with this case. Johnny definitely seemed more upbeat than Carly at this point. At least Johnny was assured of one thing; this evidence might point them toward a suspect other than Billy. Maybe the suspect was a girl. Perhaps Billy was implying that there was a girl with him in that room. One big question still remained: Who grabbed that jar, possibly trying to move it to get at those chocolate bars in Ms. Williams' purse?

As the kids headed up to Johnny's room, Mr. Copper hollered to them that they were forgetting something. He held the two notecards, which contained the prints, high in the air, waving them back and forth, trying to get their attention. "Don't forget your evidence, kids."

Carly grabbed their fingerprint evidence from Mr. Copper, and then quickly dashed toward the stairway.

"Thanks, Dad!" Johnny yelled.

"Yeah, thank you, Mr. C," Carly added. The detectives considered their newfound information to decide what they were going to do next. Fortunately, they had a whole stack of newly rolled fingerprints, which Mr. Copper said that he would look at, but not until later in the evening, after dinner. Hopefully, he would be able to make an identification of the person that grabbed that jar.

Johnny and Carly were considering their next strategic move. "Are we going to set up the undercover camera or not, Copper?" Carly asked. "I think we should."

"I have a feeling I know who our chocolate thief is, Carly." Johnny sounded sure of himself. "Even though I have a hunch, I still agree that the camera might help catch our suspect in the act."

Carly was not very thrilled with the fact that Johnny kept secret hunches from her at times. "Who do you think the suspect is, Copper? Were you planning on telling me?" she asked, folding her arms in front of her in frustration.

"I have a strong hunch that our suspect is a girl, but I'm sure her prints won't exactly match the fingerprints we found on the jar," replied Johnny. "I think the undercover video camera is going to tell us the whole story."

"You may be right, Copper," Carly admitted. "We always seem to focus our attention on the boys when things go wrong."

Johnny started laughing. "I've noticed that too. Boys seemed to get blamed for just about everything. You know what I mean?"

Carly could sense some sarcasm from Johnny, but it was true. "I guess we just usually rely on the statistics," she replied, returning some of her own sarcasm. "It's commonly known that boys get into more trouble than girls."

"You got me there. I can't argue with good old common sense," Johnny said in agreement. "But this time I think it's going to be different. The hidden camera might just tell us for sure."

"I can't wait," said Carly. "You just tell me where and when to hide the camera and I will get a hold of Ms. Williams and get it done."

"Let's plan on tomorrow if it works out with Ms. Williams' schedule," Johnny decided. "We do need to remember one thing."

"What's that, Copper?" Carly inquired.

"We can't stop searching for other clues in this case, because there is a chance the chocolate thief may never return to strike again." Johnny began to sound a little pessimistic. "If our suspect doesn't come back to steal anymore chocolate bars, our hidden camera won't do us any good."

"Copper, this investigation is draining me. Could we at least take the night off from this case and relax a little bit?" Carly suggested. She had some plans for the two detectives, and she thought Johnny would really enjoy them.

9

"Tonight is going to be relaxing and fun," Carly assured Johnny. The two were going to go to the school's fall musical, which was being presented in the auditorium. They both hoped to quit thinking about their big case and just relax for a couple of hours. *The Wizard of Oz* was this year's choice for the school musical, and it just happened to be one of Carly's all-time favorites. The drama club was very talented, and both Johnny and Carly had friends in this year's show.

They arrived at the school about a half hour before the performance in hopes of getting a front row seat. They talked for a while before settling into their chairs and had their minds completely off of the investigation. Unfortunately, the pleasant experience of simply enjoying the musical did not last very long.

Shortly into the show Johnny began to feel a sharp elbow in his ribs from Carly. She seemed to be frantically trying to get his attention. Carly was focused on a classmate that was in the musical, playing an unusual part. The actress was a girl they knew, and Shannon was her name. Shannon was playing the role of the Scarecrow this year, which seemed somewhat strange, because the role of the Scarecrow had always been portrayed by a boy in the past. Carly was noticeably anxious and squirming in her seat. Johnny was getting a little upset, because she would not sit still and watch the musical. After all, she was the one that had planned this surprise.

"Hey, Copper, check out the scarecrow," Carly stated, with obvious suspicion on her mind.

"OK … I'm checking out the scarecrow … it's Shannon," Johnny whispered, wondering where she was going with this annoying interruption. "Why are you so preoccupied with her?"

"She's the perfect little actress for the role, don't you think, Copper?" Carly waited, but received no response. "Wouldn't you agree?" Carly asked, her voice sounding more assertive. "Look at how Shannon dances and leaps, jumping around so easily."

"What about how much she jumps around?" Johnny asked, with even more impatience in his voice. "I don't know where you're going with this."

"Look at how easily she dances, jumps and leaps around," Carly said, trying to get Johnny to listen to her own hunch about the suspect in this case. "Shannon is so light on her feet, I'd bet she's a great climber, if you know what I mean, Copper."

"Don't tell me what you're thinking, Carly," Johnny warned.

"Copper, we have to consider every student in our class as a possible suspect, and I have a strong hunch about Shannon," Carly declared. "Remember what your dad said to us after he inspected our fingerprint evidence?"

"Yes, I remember," Johnny stated. "He said the prints looked like those of a child and not an adult."

"He did say child, but he also went on to say we needed to consider the girls in the class as well," Carly pointed out.

"Are you telling me you think Shannon is a possible suspect?" Johnny asked, a little shocked. "You think Shannon would steal from Ms. Williams?"

"It's just my gut feeling," Carly stated. "Shannon is a girl, and she's quite an athlete. So climbing up to the shelf would be easy."

"Is there anything else about her that makes her a suspect, though?" Johnny wondered. "There has to be more than just a hunch, don't you think?"

Carly did remember one other thing that was important. "Copper, if I'm not mistaken, Shannon and Billy are the best of friends, and she does sit right behind him in class."

Carly and Johnny had a hard time concentrating on the musical, so their evening of relaxation came to an end. Shannon, in her role as the Scarecrow, was on their minds now. She was quite small, but muscular, and was very agile, because of her training in gymnastics. She was probably the tiniest girl in school, but had more upper body strength than most of the football players. But, did this make her a good suspect? Did she have the ability to climb to that upper shelf where the chocolate was hiding? She did not look like she ate much chocolate. What about Mr. Copper's statement that the evidence may have been left by a child, and possibly a girl? These questions stormed through the minds of Johnny and Carly. Carly was really focused on Shannon now.

"Copper, remember you were talking about the suspect as a girl, right?" Carly asked.

"Yes, I did say that I thought it was a girl, but I never considered Shannon as a suspect in these thefts," Johnny replied, seemingly baffled. "Would you have ever suspected Shannon?"

"Well, to be quite honest, you've been playing a lot of games with me lately about the suspect that you've been considering, and it has been driving me a little crazy." Carly was not happy that Johnny had not been sharing his recent hunch with her.

"You know the comments you've been making. You've said things, like 'it's a *girl*' and 'I think I know who *she* is' and 'the person has to be small and a good climber.'" Carly was acting a little irritated at Johnny now.

"Hold on a minute," Johnny replied. "What does this have to do with Shannon? Do you think she could do such a thing? I never thought for a moment it was her. "

"When I saw Shannon on that stage tonight I could not help but notice her little body, strong muscles and the fact that she would be such a great climber." Carly did not hesitate to argue her point. She was making a lot of sense. "On top of all of that, Shannon is very good friends with Billy, she sits right behind him in class and he was our first suspect in this case."

"I guess you're making a lot of sense," Johnny assured Carly, starting to feel a little uncertain about his own theory of who the culprit was in this case.

"So, what do we do?" Carly asked.

"I see where you're going with this. You make a great argument, but I still think you have it wrong," Johnny said, with his confidence a little shaken. "You have to think of Shannon's personality, too. She's an angel," Johnny said, strongly defending Shannon's honesty. "If she found a quarter on the floor, she would turn it in to Ms. Williams. Don't you think so?"

"I guess you're right, Copper, but I'm just trying to solve this case, and we can't overlook anyone as a suspect." Carly was looking for some agreement from Johnny. She knew good detectives had to look at all the angles in a case. "We simply can't ignore Shannon, can we?"

"You're right. We can't. You have me second-guessing my own theory now," Johnny said, somewhat dejected.

Johnny turned to face Carly. Deep in thought, he was struggling with what to do, or say, next in this case. "Carly, I've made a decision and I need your help."

"What can I do?" she asked with enthusiasm and a desire for more work.

"You have to talk to Shannon as soon as possible," Johnny said with certainty, even though he simply could not imagine Shannon being involved in any kind of theft. "See what she knows about the missing chocolate, if anything, and then let me know what she tells you. Being close friends with Billy, she might know something."

"I'll do it, Copper," Carly answered with even more confidence than usual. "After all, I am the one that spotted her in the first place."

"Yes, you did," Johnny smirked. "Let's see what kind of interviewing skills you have. Shannon is as sharp as a tack, Carly," Johnny reminded her. "She just might turn out to be a tough nut to crack."

"Copper, would you stop using all of your dad's one-liners, like 'sharp as a tack' and 'tough nut to crack,'" Carly said as she began to tease him. "You've been imitating your dad way too much lately."

The Wizard of Oz finally came to an end, and unfortunately both detectives barely paid attention to the show. Once again, they were too preoccupied with their investigation. The hopes of relaxing for just one night would have to be postponed.

"You just concentrate on Shannon... OK, Carly?" Johnny asked as they walked out to Carly's mom's car for their ride home.

"Leave it to me," Carly replied with a noticeable quiver in her voice. Her sureness was starting to get a little shaky and Johnny knew it.

"Just do your best," Johnny encouraged. "You'll be fine."

Both kids hopped in the car and Mrs. Cruz dropped Johnny off at his house. Carly had no intention of going home, and asked her mom to drop her off at Shannon's house for a few minutes. Carly had other plans on her mind, and was her stomach ever churning now. Carly was bound and determined to interview their new suspect tonight. She could hardly wait to get to Shannon's house.

10

Carly knocked on the door at Shannon's house, hoping she was home from the musical by now. Shannon arrived quickly at the front door and greeted Carly, welcoming her inside.

"Do you have a few minutes to talk?" Carly asked.

"Sure, let's head up to my room and no one will bother us," Shannon replied.

When they got to Shannon's room, Carly could not help but notice the trophies and photographs of Shannon's gymnastic competitions. Carly began to think more and more that Shannon would have had no problem climbing to the top shelf in Ms. Williams' room.

"First, I wanted to tell you how much I enjoyed the *Wizard of Oz* tonight," Carly said. "Copper and I went together, and he really enjoyed it too."

Shannon was thankful, but somehow she could tell that discussing the musical was not the true reason Carly was there. The girls were always kind to each other, but they were not close friends.

"Hey Shannon, how well do you like Billy?" Carly blurted out.

Shannon was stunned and hesitant to answer. "Well, I'd say I like him quite a bit. He's not my best friend, but out of all the boys in class, I guess I like him the most. Why do you ask that, Carly?" Shannon wondered.

"Have you ever seen Billy go into Ms. Williams' room when no one else was around?" Carly asked, straight to the point.

"Is Billy in trouble for going into the teacher's room during recess?" Shannon questioned, clearly upset.

Carly was not even able to get another question out when Shannon began to come to Billy's defense.

"I know he didn't do anything wrong in there," Shannon claimed. "I saw him."

"You're saying that you *saw* Billy *not* do anything wrong?" Carly asked with a confused look. She had never heard anyone protect another person with that sort of logic.

"Well, I did see him in Ms. Williams' room once or maybe twice, over recess," Shannon began and then paused. "I know exactly why he was in there, Carly. I just can't talk about it, though."

"Did you *see* what he was actually doing in our classroom, or did he just *tell* you why he was in there?" Carly was trying to get Shannon to speak out, but Shannon did not seem willing to answer her questions directly.

"I guess you could say both," Shannon admitted, as if she knew precisely what Billy was doing in there. Unfortunately, Carly was not sure what Shannon was trying to confess. Shannon tried to be clearer in her explanation. "Well, I saw what he was doing and he also told me what he had been doing in there."

Shannon looked at Carly straight in the eyes, and decided to confront her. "I have a question for you, Carly. If you saw Copper doing something he was not supposed to be doing, would you tell the teacher, even if it meant he might get into trouble?" Shannon asked, putting Carly on the spot.

Carly found herself in an unusual predicament. She felt as if she were on the wrong end of the interview. Carly thought to herself: *Okay, get it together detective. Who is questioning who here? Let's turn this around, and get back in charge.*

Carly changed her questioning to get back in control of the situation. "Shannon, you like Billy a lot, don't you?"

"I guess you could say that," Shannon replied, a little embarrassed.

Carly went on. "This may sound like an obvious question, but would you cover for Billy if you saw him doing something wrong?"

Shannon looked at Carly, as if she did not want to answer that question.

"Would it be safe for me to say that Billy would cover for you if he saw you doing something wrong?" Carly asked, as if she already knew the answer.

"Yes, I guess you could say that," Shannon responded, with a scared look on her face. "I don't know exactly what you're talking about, but I would say Billy is that kind of friend."

Shannon did look confused. "What does this have to do with me seeing Billy in Ms. Williams' room anyway?" Shannon finally asked, hoping she would get Carly to tell her what was going on.

"Until you tell me what you saw Billy doing in her classroom over recess, I won't know if my questions are really important or not," Carly replied.

Because of Shannon's nervous behavior, Carly was now starting to believe that both Billy and Shannon were somehow involved in the thefts of the chocolate bars. This was difficult to imagine, because Carly respected Billy and Shannon. Carly just stared at Shannon as she looked for the right words to say. Carly considered one apparent thing as she thought to herself:

Could they have promised each other to keep the chocolate thefts a secret, even if they were confronted?

Shannon spoke up in frustration. "I would love to tell you what I saw Billy doing in Ms. Williams' room, but he made me promise to keep it to myself." It seemed like Shannon wanted to cooperate with Carly, but she just could not betray Billy.

Carly took advantage of Shannon's softening, hoping for a straightforward answer. "Have you been inside Ms. Williams' room with Billy during recess?"

"Yes... I can't lie about that. I was in there once or twice. Well... maybe even three times," Shannon finally admitted. "I just can't remember for sure, Carly."

"What were you two doing in there?" Carly asked again, hoping Shannon would finally break down and tell her the truth. "You know it's against school rules to be in there at all over recess," Carly reminded her.

"I just can't tell you why we were in there, because if I do Billy and I will get into trouble," Shannon spurted out with some relief. She seemed very worried now.

Carly felt bad that Shannon looked as if she might cry. "I'm sorry, Shannon. I didn't mean to get so pushy. That's all the questions I have for now."

Carly headed out of the bedroom and down the stairs toward the front door. Shannon followed her closely. As usual, Carly sped down the stairway two steps at a time, with little Shannon right behind her. When it came to athletics, Carly had met her match with Shannon.

"I hope we're still friends, Shannon," Carly said, knowing that she was a little rough on her during the interview.

"I'm sorry I wasn't able to tell you everything I wanted to," Shannon stated, as Carly flew out the front door. "I'm going to talk to Billy, because I think he needs to tell the whole truth about what's been going on in that classroom."

"I'm always here if you want to talk, Shannon," Carly offered, as she sprinted away. Carly lived close to Shannon, so the run home would be quick.

She was very anxious to call Johnny and tell him about the interview. She knew that he was not going to be very happy with the results.

Did I get anything out of my talk with Shannon? What was Shannon trying to tell me? Did she just see Billy steal the chocolate, or could it be that she was in on the thefts with him?

Carly thought to herself all the way home, trying to make sense out of her strange conversation with Shannon. Carly did succeed in learning one important piece of evidence. Shannon admitted being inside that classroom, two or three times, along with Billy. Questions still remained: Why was she in there? Was it for the chocolate?

Carly wished she had pulled more information out of Shannon. As she made her way home, she kept going over the facts of this case, mumbling quietly. "Without more evidence, none of my questions can be answered. Billy and Shannon will have to come forward together and talk honestly about what took place in Ms. Williams' classroom. I just hope Copper still wants me as a partner after he learns I didn't get a confession out of Shannon."

Carly made it home quickly, but her mother and father were waiting at the door to have a talk with her about a few things. One of them was Carly's lack of focus on her homework. This case had taken a lot of her attention away from school, and that was not a good thing. Carly could tell her mom and dad were ready for a serious conversation.

"Mom … Dad, I know you want to talk, and I promise to listen to you right after I call Copper," Carly bargained, with some desperation in her voice.

"Not so quick, young lady!" Mr. Cruz announced. "There will be no phone calls tonight. You will see Johnny in the morning at school."

"This can't wait, Dad. I have to call Copper with the latest news," she begged.

"No more arguing about it," Mr. Cruz demanded. "Up to your room and straight to your school work."

Carly went to her bedroom to do her homework, trying hard to keep her mind off of her strange chat with Shannon. Unfortunately for Carly, Johnny had a piece of evidence of his own that she needed desperately to hear. But that would also have to wait.

11

The next day proved to be somewhat puzzling, but still worthwhile. Carly and Johnny met privately with their teacher. It was almost 9 o'clock and the investigators met with Ms. Williams in the classroom, before other kids started coming in. Johnny told Ms. Williams that he believed they were getting close to solving the case of the thefts of her chocolate bars. Johnny updated her with the latest information.

"Ms. Williams, I don't believe that Billy is a suspect in this case anymore." Johnny knew that Ms. Williams still thought that Billy was the No. 1 suspect. What Johnny did not know was how much Carly disagreed with his opinion about Billy. Carly now believed that Billy just might be the perfect suspect. The problem was Carly still hadn't had a chance to talk to Johnny about her interview with Shannon the night before. Therefore, Carly did not know about Johnny's big news either. Carly patiently listened and did not interrupt Johnny while he gave his summary of the case to Ms. Williams.

"Are you positive about Billy?" Ms. Williams replied in shock. "I thought you were going to tell me that he was the one."

"I believe I know for sure, with 99 percent certainty, who stole your three chocolate bars," Johnny stated, quite sure of himself. He did not exactly shout out the name of his new suspect, though.

"It's always important to know for sure," Johnny cautioned. "So I'm not going to give you a name yet." He knew that accusing innocent people, without having all of the proper evidence, could be very bad for his reputation. He really wanted to be certain before he laid out his case.

Carly finally interrupted and leaned over, whispering in Johnny's ear. "We need to talk right now," demanded Carly, as she pulled Johnny to the back of the room away from Ms. Williams. "Guess what, Copper? Shannon said some things last night that just might change your mind about Billy."

Johnny turned his head and looked at Carly, as he wrinkled his eyebrows in bewilderment. "Really, that's interesting. I wish you would have called me last night."

"Sorry about that," Carly replied. "Mom and Dad have not been so happy with me lately. They wouldn't let me call you last night. I could hardly fall asleep."

"Well, I guess I could have tried to call you too," Johnny admitted. "I have some new information that will knock your socks off!"

Carly looked at Johnny with anticipation as they walked back over to Ms. Williams, hoping for a big favor. "We would like one more piece of rock-solid evidence," Johnny advised their teacher.

"With your permission, I would like to go ahead and set up the undercover camera in your room," Carly suggested, looking over at Johnny for agreement. "We think it's time for our suspect to hit again, right Copper?"

"That's right," Johnny said as he smiled in agreement.

"That's fine with me," Ms. Williams said. "I told you both to just let me know how I could help."

Carly was clearly excited. "Great! If I could get back in your room about 15 minutes before noon, I can set it up and get the camera zoomed in on your purse," Carly told Ms. Williams.

"Do you want me to put my purse in the exact same place I always do?" Ms. Williams asked.

"Yes, definitely," Johnny said. "Would you mind placing one of your favorite chocolate bars in the side pocket? I want to restage the crime scene exactly how it happened the first three times."

"That's not a problem. I have one in my desk drawer right now," replied Ms. Williams. "Johnny... how confident are you about this?" she asked.

"I'm as certain as anyone could be. Our candy thief loves chocolate, and today will be no exception," Johnny guaranteed his teacher.

Ms. Williams was getting anxious to get to the truth, but was also a little sad. Even though she wanted to get to the bottom of these crimes, she was frustrated anticipating the outcome. She was not at all happy about the fact the suspect was most likely one of her wonderful students. After being told by Johnny that Billy was no longer a suspect, she could not imagine who Johnny thought was the chocolate thief.

"I will meet you kids back here, shortly before noon. Will that work out for both of you?" Ms. Williams inquired.

"That will be perfect," Johnny responded. Neither Carly nor Johnny told Ms. Williams about Shannon. They figured it was best not to worry her anymore about her students. This case was hard enough on her. Both detectives quickly scooted out of the classroom door, heading toward their lockers, anticipating their next move.

"We'll see you then!" Carly and Johnny bellowed, responding at the exact same time, with that familiar harmony in their voices. They laughed at how their minds worked so closely together.

"Beat you to my locker, Copper," Carly challenged. She headed down the hall with her usual swiftness. Copper had learned that winning these races against Carly was just not in the cards, so he did not even attempt to catch her. All of a sudden, out jumped a hall monitor from a doorway next to Carly's locker. "Slow down, young lady!" warned the monitor, "Or you will be staying after school in detention."

"Yes, sir. I'm just a little excited this morning. Sorry," Carly softly apologized. She opened her locker and peeked out from behind the gray metal door. Johnny arrived at her locker, still moving at his classic turtle pace, with a big smirk on his face.

"What happened, Carly? Did somebody catch you running again?" Johnny questioned with a giggle. "You'll never learn, will you?"

"Speaking of learning, Copper, do you want to hear about my interview with Shannon?" Carly asked, wondering if Johnny was curious.

"Oh yeah, I almost forgot," Johnny replied. "What's up?"

"Shannon is one tough girl," Carly reported, somewhat dejected that she did not get a confession from her. "She never admitted to stealing any chocolate, but she did admit that she was in our classroom two or three times with Billy," Carly stated, anticipating Johnny's response. All she got was a blank stare from him in return.

"Is that all?" Johnny wondered, hoping for more. "That's the big news."

"What do you mean 'is that all'?" Carly snapped back. "Shannon admitted being in Ms. Williams' room, two or three times, with our main suspect, Billy."

"Did she say if she ever saw Billy steal any chocolate from Ms. Williams' purse?" Johnny asked, trying to remain calm.

Carly was cautiously proud about the information she did get out of Shannon. "No, not exactly, but she kept saying that Billy was doing something wrong while he was in the classroom. She just wouldn't say what it was."

"Shannon did ask one interesting question. She wondered if I would ever turn you in if I saw you do something wrong," Carly reported. "I told her I probably wouldn't."

Johnny just smiled. "So, you think that Shannon was trying to tell you that she witnessed Billy steal the chocolate, without coming right out and saying it?"

"What else could she have been talking about?" Carly asked.

"That's interesting. I guess I better tell you about my new piece of information, too," Johnny hesitantly replied.

"I guess you better, Copper," Carly demanded. "What's going on?"

"Dad identified the person who left the two fingerprints on that glass jar," Johnny stated in a reluctant tone.

"Tell me!" Carly shouted as she stared straight at Johnny, waiting nervously. "Come on, Copper, who is it?"

"Don't get a big head over this new evidence, but the fingerprints belong to Shannon," Johnny revealed, but not very enthusiastically.

"I told you, Copper!" Carly snapped. "This is all coming together now. Think about the evidence: They both go into the classroom. They both admitted going into the room without permission. Shannon said she watched Billy doing something wrong. And now, Shannon's fingerprints are on the glass jar, which was sitting right next to Ms. Williams' purse." Carly just gloated, believing she may have solved the case. Had she? Was it Billy and Shannon that stole the chocolate? Carly and Johnny got their books for the next class and went their separate ways.

"Meet you later," Johnny said with a bummed look on his face.

"You will if you're lucky, Copper," Carly teased as she turned to run to her next class. She took three long steps, remembered the hall monitor, and then promptly slowed down to a brisk walk. She looked over her shoulder and Johnny was watching her, shaking his head back and forth, wondering why she never learned her lesson. Luckily, the hall monitor had gone on to other problems further down the hall. Otherwise, Carly would have been staying after school.

12

Carly arrived back to the classroom at 11:45. She brought her dad's digital video camera to Ms. Williams' room where she met her teacher and Johnny. Johnny and Carly agreed on the perfect place to set up the undercover camera. It was up high on a shelf, on the opposite side of the room from where Ms. Williams' purse was to be placed for the suspect. There was a straight camera shot at Ms. Williams' purse, so Carly had to make certain the chocolate bar was placed just right in the side pocket. This was where she always carried her chocolate bars, and there could not be any change. This undercover operation had to be just like the real thing. Johnny and Carly didn't want to give the suspect any hint that something was going on. After the kids lined up for lunch, the purse was put in place. The chocolate bar was positioned perfectly, and the camera was ready to go. Just one push of the record button and the surveillance would be underway.

The two detectives and Ms. Williams waited for the bell to ring for lunch and recess. They were nervous about the operation. Would the suspect come back? After all, three thefts were pretty brave; four would really be risky. Was the suspect bold enough to return for a fourth chocolate bar? The bell rang, and all the kids were anxious to eat lunch, and then go outside for some fun. It was Ms. Williams' job to turn on the video camera after every student was gone from the room. Johnny was a little nervous that she might make a mistake and not get the camera turned on correctly. He knew that he needed to have faith in her. Everything was now in place, the video camera was ready, and

Johnny, Carly and Ms. Williams were nervously waiting, wondering, and anticipating how this investigation would come to an end.

After lunch, Ms. Williams was outside monitoring the playground. She was trying to keep one eye on Billy, since she was not totally convinced that he was no longer the main suspect. The more the time passed, the more she realized that Billy was very busy playing and talking to other kids. He did not seem to be interested in sneaking into the school.

"Maybe he's not the suspect," she quietly convinced herself. She began to ignore Billy, paying attention to the rest of the children at recess. Johnny and Carly sat down in the grass and began to discuss their case.

"Carly, I have to say that I just can't believe Billy or Shannon, and especially both of them together, would ever steal from Ms. Williams." Johnny was hopeful about his new theory, but very concerned about finding Shannon's fingerprints on the glass jar.

"You may be right, Copper, but you haven't explained some of the evidence right under our noses," Carly challenged.

"Like what?" Johnny asked.

"Copper, during my interview with Shannon she admitted to me that she and Billy entered Ms. Williams' classroom on two or three occasions," Carly stated. She knew Johnny was a 'just the facts' sort of guy. He just wanted the evidence.

"Go on, Carly," he replied.

"So why are you so certain Billy and Shannon are innocent?" Carly wondered. "Shannon told me that she and Billy were in that classroom, without permission from the teacher, doing something that they could both get into trouble for."

"But wait a minute," Johnny interrupted. "Shannon refused to tell you what it was that she and Billy were doing in there, right?"

"That's true, but why are you ignoring the fingerprints Shannon put on that jar?" Carly probed, trying to get Johnny to think straight. "Why would Shannon be up on that shelf grabbing that jar, which just happened to be in the way of the purse, where the chocolate was?" Carly's impatience was growing quickly. "Copper, you have to really believe in coincidences if you think those two were not in there for those chocolate bars."

"I believe I can explain the confusion, but I'm just not ready yet," Johnny stated, even more certain now, than ever, of what occurred in that classroom. He felt as though there were no longer good reasons to suspect Billy, or Shannon, of committing the thefts. Deep down, Johnny felt more and more confident of one suspect he had been considering for the past couple of days.

Johnny and Carly continued their playground chatter, causing them to lose their sense of time, and also lose their line of sight of both Billy and Shannon. Where were they? Where did they go?

"Cross your fingers, Carly. If the surveillance camera works, it's going to confirm my belief about Billy and Shannon," Johnny whispered, with the coolness of an experienced detective.

"Who do you suspect, Copper?" Carly demanded, reminding him that she was his one and only partner. "The curiosity is driving me crazy!"

Johnny just smiled contently, knowing he was really annoying her.

"As I said before, I want to witness one more piece of evidence and that's our video," Johnny stated. "If it turns out to be who I think it is, you will be shocked."

"I'll give you one hint, Carly," Johnny teased. "After that, you'll have to witness, for yourself, the fourth and final theft of chocolate on that video."

"What's the hint, Copper? Who are you talking about?" Carly was getting very impatient. She dreaded Johnny's ego when he felt he had solved a big case.

Johnny got up onto his feet, walked over and sat down on one of the swings. He started rocking back and forth, faster and faster, higher and higher. "Here's the hint, Carly," Johnny said as he teased her every time he swung past her.

"Go on, Copper," Carly demanded, "Before I yank you out of that swing."

Johnny swung one last time, jumped from the swing and landed on the ground with a big thud. "Here's your only clue: The suspect I have in mind was not in our classroom last year."

"Now I know for sure you're wrong, Copper," Carly said with confidence. "I know every single student in our classroom."

"Wait and see on the video, Carly," Johnny snapped back. "If the suspect returns to the old crime scene, like I believe she will, you are going to know by the end of class who I'm talking about."

This intense conversation suddenly made both Johnny and Carly lose sight of Billy and Shannon altogether. Carly looked around, unable to find either one. Then, just as quickly as she lost them, she locked her sights in on both of them again.

"Well, I can say one thing for certain, Copper," she said as she pointed toward the edge of the baseball field. "I don't know for sure who you suspect, but I know that Billy and Shannon are both sitting by the dugout over there, and they seem pretty comfortable," Carly claimed. "I haven't seen either one of them go anywhere near the school today."

"Well then, I guess there's no way it could be either of those two," Johnny gladly replied. "Didn't I just tell you it was not either one of them?"

"Don't get me wrong, Copper. I will be glad if it turns out that neither Billy nor Shannon is involved in this mess," Carly admitted. "I really like both of them and I couldn't imagine either one stealing from Ms. Williams."

Carly had an important point that she had waited to express. "Remember this, Copper. If we go back to that classroom and that chocolate bar has *not* been stolen and there's absolutely nothing on that video, you're going to be questioning yourself again about Billy and Shannon's innocence."

Johnny considered what Carly had just said. "That's very true Carly, but we will just have to wait and see."

All of a sudden, something very alarming happened. Carly spotted Billy and Shannon slowly sneaking toward the side door of the school, apparently going back to class early. They were obviously going back into school without anyone's permission.

"Copper, I think your theory is about to be ruined," Carly said, as she pointed toward Billy and Shannon.

Johnny did not reply. He just sat back and watched intently, anticipating what was going to occur next. As they sat and watched, Billy and Shannon strutted straight into the school building, acting as if they were invisible.

Carly turned to Johnny and just smiled. Johnny could not help but wonder what was about to happen.

13

Were Billy and Shannon foolish enough to go back into Ms. Williams' room to steal more chocolate? Did they have a good reason to enter the school building? Were Billy and Shannon, who seemed like great kids, about to make Johnny look like a fool? There were still about 15 minutes left of recess. Why would they want to go back inside now? Was Johnny all wrong about Billy? Did Billy lie to Johnny after all? Should Johnny have paid more attention to Carly's interview with Shannon? Maybe Shannon was involved.

Johnny began to doubt his own beliefs on how these thefts were committed. Billy and Shannon now seemed to be in on this together. All of these questions raced through Johnny's mind. There was one piece of the puzzle left, so Johnny tried to calm himself down. The video evidence would be the last hope for answers in this case.

The bell rang right at 1 o'clock, and all the kids ran to get into line so they could go back to class. Ms. Williams saw to it that everybody was behaving and calmed down before she let them walk down the hallway to her room. She winked at Carly and Johnny, as if to say that she hoped the investigation was almost over. They both just smiled back at her. None of the other kids had a clue as to what was going on. Carly still wondered which student Johnny suspected: *Perhaps there is a student that Copper suspects, but he is simply confused about where this person went to school last year. Could this be possible? Copper has to be smarter than that. What is Copper thinking? Who does he suspect of doing these crimes?*

Johnny had already told Carly to disregard Shannon, but Carly was convinced he was wrong. She knew that Shannon had something to confess, but what was it? Her strange behavior and strong defense of Billy during her interview had to mean something in this case. Shannon's prints on that jar were very difficult to explain considering the jar sat right next to Ms. Williams' purse.

All of the students reached the classroom and plopped down in their desks to get ready for class. Ms. Williams had a lot of afternoon paperwork to do, and she gave all of the kids a writing assignment to keep them busy.

Ms. Williams approached her two detectives. "Excuse me, Carly and Johnny, could you help me with some things in the back of the room?"

"Yes, Ms. Williams," they both replied together.

Ms. Williams walked to the back of the room as they followed. She led them into a very tiny equipment room. They squeezed into the cramped room, more like a big closet, where a TV and other electronics sat on a little table. The three of them were able to talk quietly, so the other kids couldn't hear what was going on.

"I want you kids to know something," Ms. Williams said. "I looked up on the shelf as I came in from recess, and I can already see that my purse has been moved." Both kids became very jittery as Ms. Williams spoke. "I am sure the chocolate bar is missing."

Carly looked at Johnny as he peered back at her. He seemed awfully calm, but Carly knew him very well and was sure his stomach was churning with uncertainty. Both of the young detectives knew this case was finally solved. Unless the video camera malfunctioned, the suspect was about to be revealed.

"I guess the video is going to answer all of our questions," Johnny said. Carly felt bad for Johnny. She knew that it was difficult for him to believe Billy or Shannon could have committed these thefts. She just couldn't get over the fact that when she thought back on Copper's interview with Billy and her interview with Shannon, both suspects behaved the exact same way. Guilty!

Ms. Williams whispered another curious finding. "I found the wrapper to my chocolate bar on the floor, right in between Billy's and Shannon's desks."

"I just don't see how that can be!" Johnny reacted, loud enough to cause a commotion with the other students in class. Ms. Williams quickly quieted the kids back down and told them to return to their writing assignment.

"Well, I know it was, because I saw it there when we walked into the room and I went straight to it and picked it up," Ms. Williams replied as she pulled the wrapper from her pocket, handing it over to Carly. Sure enough, the wrapper, no longer containing chocolate, had been found. That made it theft No. 4.

Johnny began to feverishly reexamine all of the evidence over and over again in his mind: *Why is it that when we suspected Billy of the first three thefts, Ms. Williams had never found any of the candy bar wrappers near his desk? Is it because he picked them up and threw them away? Mr. Miller said he saw Billy with one of the wrappers. But now, just when I'm convinced Billy could not have possibly stolen the fourth chocolate bar, the wrapper is found right on the floor near his desk?*

Ms. Williams began to seek answers herself. "Let's consider Mr. Miller again for a moment. He says that he witnessed Billy in the room during at least one of the thefts. That means that he admits that he was in the area of the thefts. Maybe Mr. Miller is not telling the truth about Billy, just to cover for himself."

Ms. Williams and Carly looked at each other, and then over at Johnny, hoping these questions would be answered shortly.

Johnny began to speak and assured Carly and their teacher that he was now certain about who committed these crimes. "It's not Billy or Shannon, and it certainly was not Mr. Miller. The video is going to prove it."

Carly just stared at him in total confusion. Ms. Williams quietly walked past the other students, dreading what was about to occur. She went to the shelf where the hidden camera sat. She used a small stepladder to reach the shelf, grabbed the camera and walked it back to the small room where Carly and Johnny waited patiently. Carly took the video camera from her teacher and connected it directly to the TV for their secret viewing. None of the other students paid attention to Ms. Williams. She was always walking around the classroom picking things up, putting things away and doing small odd jobs while the kids read or did homework. When it came to Johnny and Carly, they paid strict attention to Ms. Williams.

"Well Johnny, here is your chance to tell me who it is before the camera reveals the culprit." Carly again hounded Johnny as if she were challenging him for an answer. "Is it Billy or Shannon, or did they do the crimes together?" Carly asked for the final time.

"Are you ready to learn the truth, Carly?" Johnny whispered.

"I don't want you to think I have lost any respect for you, as a detective, but you didn't listen to the clue I gave you earlier," Johnny stated, giggling. "You seemed to ignore it altogether."

"I did ignore it, because it didn't make any sense!" Carly snapped back. "There are no new students in our class. They were all here last year."

"I never said 'student,'" Johnny whispered. "I said our suspect was not in our classroom last year."

"Our suspect was not in the classroom?" Carly abruptly questioned, as she began to raise her voice.

Johnny snickered quietly, but mischievously. "Just watch the video, Detective Cruz."

The video began to roll. It was focused directly on Ms. Williams' purse. Minutes went by. Nothing happened. More time passed, and the video stayed focused directly on the purse, as it sat there on the shelf. The picture screen on the TV was clear and bright. Nothing happened for the first 15 minutes of the recording. There was no sign of a single soul on that video. Nothing or no one appeared anywhere near her purse.

Johnny fast-forwarded the digital camera until 20 minutes went by and then 30. As the three of them watched patiently, they began to hear a rustling noise. There were sounds of someone moving, which could be faintly heard in the background, but there was still no sign of the suspect on the TV screen.

About 40 minutes into the hour long video, there was a loud sudden clatter made by someone, or something. The suspect had begun to get louder and louder, seemingly getting closer and closer to their teacher's purse. Was the suspect about to appear in the picture? The anticipation was rising. They all realized for the first time that this would have been approximately the same time that Billy and Shannon were witnessed going into the school.

With only 10 minutes to go, it happened. Something occurred on the video that Ms. Williams and Carly obviously dreaded. Two voices began to speak, as the investigators and their teacher listened intently. The voices of Billy and Shannon became noticeable. They were quietly whispering to each other, which would be expected of two people who were about to commit their fourth crime. Identifying their voices was easy. Ms. Williams and Carly seemed to slump with sadness, but Johnny appeared less concerned.

Carly looked straight at Johnny. "C'mon, Copper, that is definitely Shannon's voice." She shrugged her shoulders up and down as if to say, *I told you so.*

"I don't believe Shannon would ever be involved in these thefts," Ms. Williams said as she wiped her eyes with a tissue. The voices were obviously Shannon's and Billy's. Billy quietly spoke to Shannon. They engaged in a conversation that was unusual. It was hard to figure out what they were saying. Their words were too muffled to understand. Then, the two began to speak louder. Their words became clearer.

"Where is she?" Billy asked Shannon, as if they were looking for a third person in the room.

"She's gone, Billy!" Shannon yelled with panic in her voice.

Ms. Williams and Carly were intrigued, but still clueless as to what was happening on the video. Carly looked over at Johnny, and he seemed quite pleased about what he was hearing on the video. He did not seem as worried about their conversation, which was unfolding right in front of them. The video, which seemed to be building a good case against Billy and Shannon, did not seem to be affecting Johnny at all. It was as if he expected to hear their voices. He was cool and calm.

"What's up with you, Copper?" Carly asked, annoyed at his lack of concern. "Remember your speech about the final piece of this puzzle," she continued. "The video surveillance was going to lock this case up and catch the criminals, right?"

"Well, here we are!" Carly exclaimed. "First, we thought it was Billy, and we convinced ourselves we were wrong. Then we considered Shannon, and you convinced me we were wrong."

Johnny interrupted Carly. "Remember what you always tell me? Be patient."

"My patience is gone in this case, Copper," Carly said, showing her frustration. "We may not like the ending to this case, but things don't always turn out the way detectives want, right?"

"I agree, Carly, but this video isn't over with yet," Johnny quietly replied, remaining calm.

The three of them continued to watch the video as it unfolded. Billy's voice rang out loudly now. "There she is, Shannon. Up there!"

Johnny began to smile as he watched Carly and Ms. Williams staring at the television. Ms. Williams and Carly overheard Johnny whisper quietly: "I knew it. I knew it was her."

The two detectives and their teacher heard a rustling sound caused from quick movement and a rapid scurrying that neither Billy, nor Shannon, was capable of making.

Finally, the true suspect appeared at Ms. Williams' purse for one more chocolate bar. It was none other than Susie. The little thief was fast. They watched and giggled as Susie lifted the chocolate bar from the side pocket of Ms. Williams' purse, and scurried away out of the view of the camera. The little furry criminal drew smiles from the faces of Ms. Williams and both detectives. How could anyone be upset with the most popular visitor they had ever had in their classroom?

"Susie?" Carly asked, stunned. "Really…Susie?"

"I knew it was Susie," said Johnny. "I came to realize yesterday that she was our only suspect."

"Why didn't you tell me, Copper?" Carly wondered.

"I didn't want to jump to any conclusions, so I thought I'd let the video speak for me," Johnny answered. "I knew for sure that I didn't have the interviewing skills to get a confession from Susie," Johnny laughed. "After all, she is just a ring-tailed mongoose."

Carly's shoulders dropped as she felt relief that Susie was the little chocolate bar thief and not one of her classmates.

"And she sure loves chocolate, just like anyone in that classroom would love a good chocolate bar… or two… or three… or maybe four," Johnny stated, beginning to cackle.

Ms. Williams and the two detectives continued to watch the remainder of the video in disbelief. Susie the mongoose was able to easily scramble up to the top shelf, gently open up the side pouch of Ms. Williams' purse with her little nose and grab the chocolate bar. As fast as she arrived on to the scene of the crime, Susie disappeared with her stolen treat. And even though none of them could actually see her scramble away, they could hear her on the video scamper back down toward her cage. From the sounds of the voices of Billy and Shannon, Susie ran straight back to her cage, with one intention: to enjoy her favorite treat, chocolate.

Suddenly the bell rang and all the kids hurried to put their books away and head to math class. Johnny and Carly returned to their seats as well and grabbed their backpacks. Off to their next class they went, looking at each other with relief and satisfaction for solving another case. As they left the classroom, Ms. Williams thanked them both for their diligent detective work. They could tell that Ms. Williams was so happy that Susie was the chocolate thief and not one of her precious students.

When Carly and Johnny turned to walk away from their teacher, both kids felt someone tugging at their backpacks. As they turned and looked behind them, Ms. Williams was slipping one of her favorite chocolate bars into each of the detectives' backpacks. Johnny and Carly smiled at her as if to say *thanks for the reward* and then started walking to their next class. They walked faster and faster, Carly moving ahead of Johnny by two steps and then three, as she broke into a mad dash.

Johnny just stopped and began to walk. It was just not possible for him to out run his buddy, Carly. He did get the last laugh, when all of a sudden the hall monitor stepped out from behind a classroom door and brought Carly to an abrupt stop once again. The monitor's stare communicated his daily message to her: *Slow down young lady!* Carly knew that stare and quickly began walking like the rest of the kids. Well, at least for the time being. She looked back at her best friend and Johnny was just smiling, like usual.

14

At the end of the school day, Carly waited patiently for Johnny by the exit doors for their walk home together.

"Hey, Copper, give me a break down on the evidence in this case. How did you figure it out?" Carly asked.

"Well, this is how all the pieces of the puzzle finally came together," Johnny said with a sense of pride. "We had three thefts of chocolate bars, right?"

"Yeah, that's right," Carly agreed.

"They all took place in a three-week period," Johnny said, reciting the facts. "The chocolate was high on the shelf, but even this height would be a very easy climb for a ring-tailed mongoose. Mr. Miller really did not see anything of significance. He only witnessed Billy violating one of our school's policies, but he never witnessed Billy stealing anything."

"So, it *is* true that Mr. Miller witnessed Billy doing something wrong," Carly noted, "But, it only appeared that Billy was involved in the theft, because of the wrapper he was holding. I guess you could say that Billy was caught by the janitor in the wrong place at the wrong time?"

"You're exactly right, Carly," Johnny continued. "Billy had been going out for recess, just like every other student, but he was sneaking back into Ms. Williams' classroom. He was breaking the rules, sure, but he could not resist petting and playing with Susie. He had become good friends with her, because he was the one that sat right next to her cage during class. Susie felt comfortable with him sitting right beside her. One day when Billy was done playing with Susie, Mr. Miller must have seen him coming out of the room. Mr. Miller didn't think anything was wrong. He probably assumed that Ms. Williams had sent Billy into her classroom for a good reason," Johnny figured.

Detective Copper was trying to place all of the building blocks of the crime together for his partner. "You see, Carly, even before Billy started sneaking into the classroom to visit Susie, she had already learned how to get out of her cage. Look closely at the latch on the cage door, and you'll find that it's bent enough to open with a little push. Susie would get out, climb up to the top shelf, and search for that sweet smell of chocolate that she knew was in Ms. Williams' purse. Once found, she snatched it and returned to her cage to enjoy her sweet, sugary snack. By the time Billy snuck into the classroom to play with Susie, he found the empty wrappers on the floor next to his desk, because Susie was dropping them there."

"Why didn't Billy tell Ms. Williams about the candy wrappers he was finding?" Carly wondered. "That may have solved these thefts sooner."

"Think about that just for a minute, Carly," Johnny said as he tried to get her to focus. "Billy couldn't tell Ms. Williams, because then she would have determined that Billy was sneaking into the classroom during recess to play with Susie."

"I guess you're right," Carly realized. "It was his little secret, huh?"

"It sure was," Johnny explained. "This little secret was something Billy had to keep to himself. He had to keep his knowledge about the candy bar wrappers quiet or he'd get in big trouble for sneaking into Ms. Williams' room."

"Do you think Billy even knew the wrappers were being dropped there by Susie?" Carly asked. "He must have wondered where they were coming from."

"I don't think Billy ever knew for sure that it was Susie dropping the wrappers next to his desk, until the final theft of candy bar No. 4," Johnny explained. "That's the one we have on video. I don't believe Billy ever actually saw Susie stealing Ms. Williams' chocolate. He was just there to play with her."

Carly listened intently, trying to fully understand how the evidence was fitting together. "What was he doing with the wrappers?"

Johnny went on: "Billy was simply picking up the candy bar wrappers and throwing them in the garbage without thinking much about it. He had no idea where the wrappers were coming from, at first. Billy certainly never expected Susie was dropping them there, until the fourth and final theft. He definitely would have seen her dropping that one, because he and Shannon walked right in on the theft. You also have to remember that no one in our class, including Billy or Shannon, ever knew about the stolen chocolate. We were the only two, other than Ms. Williams."

"How did Susie pull this off so smoothly, Copper?" Carly wondered aloud. She was hardly able to keep from smiling at the thought of this tiny, hairy gal committing four thefts.

"Remember the first time we met Susie? Jim Walker explained that the ring-tailed mongoose has very long sharp claws that can tear their way into things," Johnny reminded her. "The mongoose is also a great climber. That little jaunt up to the top shelf was very easy for little Susie. She could out climb anyone in this school. So getting to the chocolate was no problem."

"Yeah, but what drew her to the chocolate in the first place?" Carly asked, as if she didn't understand the amazing appeal of chocolate.

"Well, I'm surprised at you for asking that question," Johnny replied, laughing at the thought of it. "You like chocolate, don't you, Carly?"

"Yes, of course I do. I love it!" Carly responded. "But I'm a kid. I'm supposed to love chocolate."

Johnny just laughed at what he thought should be very obvious. "I love chocolate too. Why shouldn't Susie like chocolate, just because she is a mongoose? If you remember what Mr. Walker said, the ring-tailed mongoose has a big sweet tooth. Susie really likes fruit, because of the sweet natural sugar."

"Oh yeah, I remember that now, Copper. So, you think she started to smell the sugar in the chocolate bars?" Carly wondered.

"You got it. Susie got a whiff of the chocolate, and she was determined to get out of that cage and find a way up to Ms. Williams' purse," Johnny explained.

"So how come she never got out of her cage during class?" Carly asked.

"I believe that when all of us kids were there, with her, she was too nervous to try and get out," Johnny assumed. "She just quietly rested in her cage."

"Do you think she was smart enough to patiently wait in her cage for us to leave?" Carly pondered.

"Yep…Susie is no dummy. She figured out that the little lever on her cage was easy to open. Just by using the tip of her nose, she pushed the latch upward about a half inch and the cage door opened for her."

"I see now," Carly said, still slightly confused. "Then she pushed the cage door open with her nose or front paw and crawled out?"

"That's right. Then Susie made her way across the table and jumped to Ms. Williams' desk and then up to the shelf. Once she made it to the purse and got the chocolate bar, she simply climbed back down and returned to her cage. The cage was where she felt safe, so she could lie down and enjoy the sweet chocolate," Johnny explained.

"So what you're saying is that Susie felt protected in her cage, so she always returned to her little home after she stole the chocolate? Is that it, Copper?" Carly asked.

"That's it!" Johnny stated.

"I have one more question that needs clearing up, Copper." Carly felt confident she would stump Johnny on this one.

"Go ahead, Carly, what is it?" Johnny smiled as if he already knew the answer.

Carly leaned toward Johnny. "Once Susie dropped the wrapper on the floor next to Billy's desk and crawled back in her open cage, how did she close the cage door and re-latch the lock?" Carly looked at Johnny as if she were challenging his intelligence. She knew this was a tough one even for him.

"Excellent question, detective, but that answer is actually quite simple. Susie did not have to shut the cage door or re-latch the lock," Johnny stated with certainty, waiting for her response.

"What do you mean, Copper? We know the lock was latched," Carly replied with confidence, believing she had Johnny cornered now. "Whenever we returned to class after recess, that cage door was always closed and locked."

Johnny was not at all stumped and continued with his line of reasoning. "Susie never cared if the cage door was closed and locked. After all, she is still just a ring-tailed mongoose. She doesn't care about levers and latches. Susie relied on her best friend to close the door and latch the lock for her."

"You mean Billy?" Carly said beginning to understand what actually happened in that classroom.

Johnny painted an entire picture of Susie's crimes, explaining the three-week mystery. "Billy locked the cage for Susie. You see, Billy had a secret, and he couldn't let it out. His secret was that he was petting and playing with Susie when he didn't have our teacher's permission. He knew he was not allowed to be anywhere near Ms. Williams' classroom during recess. Billy also knew that he certainly was not permitted to be petting and playing with Susie outside of her cage. But, Billy was not able to tell anyone about the wrappers on the floor or the fact that he was the one locking the cage after Susie returned."

"But he did tell someone," Carly noted.

"You're right. He did eventually confide in one good friend," Johnny agreed.

"You mean Shannon, right?" Carly asked.

"Right. Once Shannon got involved, she and Billy stuck together and kept their playtime with Susie their little secret. It seemed harmless."

Johnny continued his explanation: "Billy would come into the room and find Susie in the cage, but the cage door was always slightly open. He was not aware that Susie had already escaped, climbed up to the top shelf, grabbed the chocolate bar, and returned to her little home for her snack. He would just play with Susie for a while, petting and talking to her. When he was done, he locked up the cage, so no one would notice he had been there. Billy was never even sure why the cage

90

door was open. He probably figured it was just a loose lock and that Susie had bumped into it enough to shake it open."

"So, Billy didn't want to make a fuss out of the cage door?" Carly asked. "He didn't want to stir up any suspicion, right?"

"Right... Billy was not about to ask anyone, especially Ms. Williams, about the cage door, or he would get himself in trouble. He never caught Susie outside of the cage, until the final crime. This was when he and Shannon were caught talking on the video. Neither Billy nor Shannon had ever witnessed Susie eating the chocolate bars, until the fourth and final theft. They had to have caught her with the chocolate on that one; they just didn't care or even think twice about it. Billy even forgot to pick up the wrapper near his desk. That was the one Ms. Williams found. In her mind, that definitely made Billy the culprit."

"Billy must have been worried about getting caught," Carly added. "Why do you think he decided to tell Shannon?"

"I could be wrong, but I have a pretty good idea," Johnny said. "I believe that during the first couple of visits, Billy went into Ms. Williams' room alone. He confided in his friend, Shannon, maybe to impress her. After that, Shannon wanted to go in with Billy and play with Susie too, so they snuck in there together a few times. Shannon was not in on Billy's adventures from the very beginning though. "

"I totally get it now, Copper," Carly said, as if she fully grasped the entire case in her mind. "Because of his secret playtime with Susie, Billy was scared to tell anyone, except Shannon. He thought Shannon would like him more if he let her in on it."

"Bingo!" Johnny answered, as if he was finally successful in laying out the proof in this case.

"One more piece of evidence has me confused, Copper," Carly admitted, with a bewildered look. "How do you explain Shannon's fingerprints on that glass jar? We did all that work finding those prints. I thought that finally wrapped up our case, making her a clear-cut suspect."

Johnny grinned, and then answered. "Well, those fingerprints turned out to be quite innocent after all."

"What do you mean?" Carly wondered, "Fingerprints have solved a lot of criminal cases, haven't they?"

"They sure have, but they have cleared a lot of innocent people, too," Johnny reminded.

"What do you mean, Copper?" Carly asked.

"Well, I was convinced Shannon grabbed that jar sometime in the past, long before the thefts ever occurred, so I simply asked Ms. Williams a very easy question; who placed that jar up on the shelf," Johnny explained. "Ms. Williams at first had a hard time remembering, but then she recalled that a few months earlier *she* had moved that jar to the shelf. When she did, she climbed up the stepladder and asked Shannon to hand her the jar."

"How does she remember that it was Shannon?" Carly asked.

"She remembered it was Shannon who grabbed the jar, because it was sitting right next to her desk. Ms. Williams asked Shannon to hand it up to her," Johnny replied.

"So, Shannon hands the jar to Ms. Williams, and Ms. Williams places it on the shelf," Carly acknowledged.

"This was how Shannon's prints got on the jar. Her prints have been on that jar for months now," Johnny explained. "And that is how innocent people are cleared by fingerprints."

"What a simple, and innocent, explanation," Carly replied, as she laughed to herself. "I guess finding someone's fingerprints on something doesn't always mean they are guilty."

"You got that right, Carly," Johnny concluded.

"It's funny now to think of Susie eating all that chocolate," Carly said with a laugh. "I always wondered why she laid so quietly in the corner of her cage licking her paws. She seemed so happy."

Johnny giggled. "I just thought she was very fussy about her bathing habits. She was really licking her paws to get every last bit of the sugar."

"Yeah, Copper, I could just picture you lying in your bed licking chocolate off of your ugly toes! You would be all lazy and giddy, stuffed with all that messy chocolate," Carly snorted as she chuckled, then started to run away.

"You know you can't catch me, Copper!" she shouted as she took off like a bolt of lightning.

"I know I can't! Go ahead and leave me behind. I'm used to it," Johnny admitted.

Johnny then smiled from ear to ear with a devious, exaggerated grin. He was laughing to himself, knowing that right before Carly took off running he had decided to imitate Susie and quickly snatched her chocolate bar from the rear pocket of her backpack. Carly never even noticed, since she was in such a hurry. Johnny just waved goodbye as Carly sprinted away, without her chocolate bar from Ms. Williams. Johnny believed he now had two chocolate bars; one in his pocket and one in his backpack.

"See you tomorrow, Carlita!" he roared.

Johnny giggled and thought of a good prank to pull on Carly. He went over the plan in his head: *Now that I'm going to have both chocolate bars at my house tonight, I'll call Carly later to invite her over for chocolate and tell her to bring hers. She'll realize her chocolate bar is missing. Then I'll ask her if Susie was anywhere near her backpack. That will get her to run over here as fast as she can.*

Unfortunately, like always, Johnny's little prank would never work on Carly, because she was too smart for him. What Johnny didn't realize was that Carly had already pulled a *Susie-like* prank on him. Before Carly dashed away, she snuck into the rear pocket of Johnny's backpack and took his chocolate bar. Carly just laughed as she ran home, not realizing her chocolate bar was missing from her backpack. She planned on pulling the same trick on Johnny once she got to her house, but it would never work. Thankfully, for both of them their little pranks ended up totally backfiring.

Both detectives each got a big shock when they got to their homes. Johnny had the one chocolate bar he took from Carly and Carly had the one she took from Johnny. What they couldn't figure out was why the pockets of their backpacks were empty. Both of them were certain they should have two. Johnny and Carly stopped and thought for a minute, just like detectives, about what had just happened. Since they thought so much alike, it only took a short time to realize that they had been pranked by each other.

At least they both ended up with one chocolate bar as a reward for a job well done. Even more than the taste of good chocolate, Johnny Copper and Carly Cruz really enjoyed the great taste of success. As loyal partners and best friends, they worked as a team until they solved the case of the missing chocolate.

Johnny Copper's Life Lessons

1. **Don't jump to conclusions.** Make sure you have the facts about things before you come to a decision on what to believe. If you think someone has done something wrong, it is better to look at the evidence and not listen to rumors. Rumors are false statements spread by people who just don't know the truth. Patience will keep you from jumping to conclusions. How many of your friends have accused you of saying or doing something wrong, but you know that you didn't? My dad told me an important old saying, "Think before you speak!" It means that you shouldn't speak too quickly, especially when you are going to accuse someone of something. You just may be wrong. Be patient with your friends, teachers and family. Even if there are times that you may be right, it does not mean shouting it to the world is the best move you can make. Patiently studying the situation is smart. Remember, "Think before you speak!"

2. **Never, ever, steal from anyone.** That also means you should never steal from stores, businesses or people's homes and other property. Stealing is one of the worst things you can do. Always work hard to keep a good reputation. Just think if someone stole from you. It would be hard to trust them again. Trust is one of the most important things in a friendship. Honesty and integrity

builds trust, and trust builds character. You will be successful in life with good character.

3. **Take special care of your friends**, like Carly and I do. Good friends are not easy to come by. You have to have the type of friends that you can respect. In order to respect a friend, you must be a person that can be respected in return. Treat your friends like you would want to be treated. Never put your friends in a tough spot, by trying to talk them into doing something that you know is wrong. That also means you should not let your friends talk you into doing something that you know is wrong. Be proud that you can think for yourself, and that you don't always go along with the crowd. Good friends keep each other out of trouble, by encouraging one another to always do the right thing. Carly and I try to show you how good friends treat each other. As you remember from the story, although we love to tease each other, we would never hurt one another. Good friends care about each other. Until next time, keep paying attention and doing the right thing, detectives!

Your
friend,
Johnny
Copper

ABOUT THE AUTHOR

Gregory S. Heist is a retired police Captain from the Moline Police Department, located in the Quad Cities, Illinois. He has a wife and two sons. He worked for over 30 years with Moline, serving a majority of his career in the criminal investigation division. Greg also spent several years as the supervisor in charge of the community oriented policing program, with a special interest in making sure the department maintained a strong connection to the Boys and Girls Club of Moline. He retired from law enforcement in 2011.

Greg graduated from Illinois State University (Normal, Il.) in 1979 with a Bachelor of Science degree in Criminal Justice. He received a Master of Organizational Leadership degree in 2004 from St. Ambrose University (Davenport, Iowa) and graduated from the F.B.I. National Academy (Quantico, Va.) in 2006. His emphasis at the Moline Police Department was mentoring leadership and improving the management skills of future supervisors within the organization.

His purpose for the book is simple. Children who enjoy reading become more curious about the world. Reading, plus leading, equals succeeding.